THE FOLGER LIBRARY SHAKESPEARE

Designed to make Shakespeare's classic plays available to the general reader, each edition contains a reliable text with modernized spelling and punctuation, scene-by-scene plot summaries, and explanatory notes clarifying obscure and obsolete expressions. An interpretive essay and accounts of Shakespeare's life and theater form an instructive preface to each play.

Louis B. Wright, General Editor, was the Director of the Folger Shakespeare Library from 1948 until his retirement in 1968. He is the author of *Middle-Class Culture in Elizabethan England, Religion and Empire, Shakespeare for Everyman,* and many other books and essays on the history and literature of the Tudor and Stuart periods.

Virginia Lamar, Assistant Editor, served as research assistant to the Director and Executive Secretary of the Folger Shakespeare Library from 1946 until her death in 1968. She is the author of *English Dress in the Age of Shakespeare* and *Travel and Roads in England,* and coeditor of William Strachey's *Historie of Travell into Virginia Britania.*

The Folger Shakespeare Library

The Folger Shakespeare Library in Washington, D.C., a research institute founded and endowed by Henry Clay Folger and administered by the Trustees of Amherst College, contains the world's largest collection of Shakespeareana. Although the Folger Library's primary purpose is to encourage advanced research in history and literature, it has continually exhibited a profound concern in stimulating a popular interest in the Elizabethan period.

GENERAL EDITOR

LOUIS B. WRIGHT

Director, Folger Shakespeare Library, 1948–1968

ASSISTANT EDITOR

VIRGINIA A. LaMAR

Executive Secretary, Folger Shakespeare Library, 1946–1968

The Folger Library General Reader's Shakespeare

Love's Labor's Lost

by

WILLIAM SHAKESPEARE

WASHINGTON SQUARE PRESS
PUBLISHED BY POCKET BOOKS
New York London Toronto Sydney Tokyo

A Washington Square Press Publication of
POCKET BOOKS, a division of Simon & Schuster Inc.
1230 Avenue of the Americas, New York, NY 10020

ISBN: 0-671-66921-4

First Washington Square Press printing November 1961

13 12 11 10 9 8 7

Printed in the U.S.A.

Preface

This edition of *Love's Labor's Lost* is designed to make available a readable text of one of Shakespeare's most popular plays. In the centuries since Shakespeare many changes have occurred in the meanings of words, and some clarification of Shakespeare's vocabulary may be helpful. To provide the reader with necessary notes in the most accessible format, we have placed them on the pages facing the text that they explain. We have tried to make these notes as brief and simple as possible. Preliminary to the text we have also included a brief statement of essential information about Shakespeare and his stage. Readers desiring more detailed information should refer to the books suggested in the references, and if still further information is needed, the bibliographies in those books will provide necessary clues to the literature of the subject.

The early texts of all of Shakespeare's plays provide only inadequate stage directions, and it is conventional for modern editors to add many that clarify the action. Such additions, and additions to entrances, are placed in square brackets.

All illustrations are from material in the Folger Library collections.

L. B. W.
V. A. L.

July 15, 1961

Preface

This edition of *Love's Labor's Lost* is designed to make available a readable text of one of Shakespeare's most popular plays. In the centuries since Shakespeare many changes have occurred in the meanings of words, and some clarification of Shakespeare's vocabulary may be helpful. To provide the reader with necessary notes in the most accessible format, we have placed them on the pages facing the text that they explain. We have tried to make these notes as brief and simple as possible. Preliminary to the text we have also included a brief statement of essential information about Shakespeare and his stage. Readers desiring more detailed information should refer to the books suggested in the references, and if still further information is needed, the bibliographies in those books will provide necessary clues to the literature of the subject.

The early texts of all of Shakespeare's plays provide only inadequate stage directions, and it is conventional for modern editors to add many that clarify the action. Such additions, and additions to entrances, are placed in square brackets.

All illustrations are from material in the Folger Library collections.

L. B. W.
V. A. L.

July 25, 1961

A Play of Genial Raillery

Of all Shakespeare's comedies, none has been the subject of more debate than *Love's Labor's Lost.* Scholars have been unable to agree about its date, its purpose, its sources, or even its merits. An older generation of scholars argued that it was one of Shakespeare's earliest plays, if not indeed the first work of his apprenticeship. That view is no longer held, for it is obviously a sophisticated play which no neophyte could have written, and it reflects the literary and social milieu of fashionable London. It was also obviously written for an aristocratic audience and not for the public playhouse. As an "occasional" drama, it may have been designed for performance before the Queen at some great house where she was being entertained. No indisputable evidence, however, fixes the time, place, or occasion. This play remains enveloped in a mystery which fascinates scholars with conjectures and theories to assert, but it is likely to continue to baffle them until some definite evidence, as yet undiscovered, turns up to provide a substantial platform for their suppositions.

Although Hazlitt declared that *Love's Labor's Lost* was the one comedy of Shakespeare's that we could most easily spare, it apparently was a success in its day, and it has been acted with some success in our own time. The writer of these lines once saw a performance from the topmost gallery of the Old Vic theatre in London. The occupants of the gallery that particular evening were not students or sophisticates but plain citizens of London who had come for entertainment. Some of them doubtless thought that the playwright was an author still alive somewhere in the West End. They were not disappointed in the play. In fact, they were vastly amused, and the street sweeper who sat on my right nudged me from time to time and exclaimed, "That's a good 'un." What amused him and his colleagues of the top gallery was the byplay of the comic characters, Holofernes, Sir Nathaniel, Armado, Dull, Costard, and the others. For reasons inexplicable, the puns, the Latin phrases, and the wordplay, accompanied as they were with a certain amount of slapstick, delighted them. For them, the play was a success. Their reaction provides the academic critic with food for thought. All comedy is not a matter of rational appeal. Laughter in the theatre develops a kind of infection that sometimes defies explanation. *Love's Labor's Lost*, on this occasion at least, developed that kind of infectious laughter. It doubtless pleased its earliest audiences for this and other reasons.

Language held a tremendous interest for the Elizabethans, who were not afraid to experiment with both diction and style. Before Shakespeare had become a popular dramatist, Sir Philip Sidney had written his *Arcadia*, a romance full of high-sounding words, involved metaphors and similes, and thickly sprinkled allusions to classical mythology. Another innovator in style and diction was John Lyly, who first published in 1578 his *Euphues, the Anatomy of Wit*, which had at least seventeen editions by 1636. Its sequel, *Euphues and His England* (1580) was also extremely popular, requiring at least a dozen editions by 1609. These were prose novels, written in a style as distinctive as it was artificial but illustrative nevertheless of the contemporary interest in fine language, fancifully turned phrases, long, balanced sentences, figures of speech from unnatural natural history, and other stylistic peculiarities which other writers found easy to imitate or to satirize. Sidney and Lyly, of course, were not the only innovators in language and style. Edmund Spenser, in *The Shepherd's Calendar* (1579), which went through six or more editions by 1617, achieved some of his effects with conscious archaisms and demonstrated a remarkable interest in words, both old and new. Even the writers of popular pamphlets did not hesitate to invent words and to indulge in fanciful expressions. Writers occasionally fell into verbal excess that bordered on the absurd. A belated Elizabethan, Nathaniel Ward, who strayed to Massachusetts Bay, illustrated in *The Simple Cobbler of Aggawam* (1647) the long-continued vitality of this love of language for its own sake. In *Love's Labor's Lost* Shakespeare could utilize the fashionable linguistic tricks of the day and at the same time poke fun at some of the absurdities.

Pedantry is an ancient affliction of mankind, and ever since Aristophanes it has been the object of comic treatment on the stage. The pedant was a stock character in Roman comedy, and on the Italian stage of the Renaissance he made a frequent appearance. He was also indigenous in England, so that Shakespeare did not necessarily have to go to Italy for a prototype of Holofernes. Perhaps he saw in Gabriel Harvey, a contemporary, some of the pomposities of the learned pedant that he held up to ridicule in *Love's Labor's Lost.*

As a rising young writer for the stage, Shakespeare was inescapably familiar with the literary fashions of his day and with members of his craft in the literary milieu of London. His plays all demonstrate their author's capacity for keen perception of character, his unfailing ear for the nuances of contemporary language, his awareness of the world about him, and his ability to assimilate and utilize historical and social material for his purposes. In *Love's Labor's Lost* Shakespeare reflects the attitudes, the foibles, the gossip, and the peculiarities, not only of the literary coterie of London, but also of the fashionable world of the court. His play is a genial and good-natured satire of the follies of this world, written to amuse and entertain an aristocratic audience who would be expected to recognize familiar types, if not indeed certain individuals, as the butts of jests in the play. The passage of time has destroyed beyond hope of recovery the key to much of the topical allusion in the play, but we can be certain that the contemporary audience found much to laugh at that is lost to us.

But even though the comedy of topical reference

can no longer charm us, Shakespeare in this, as in his later plays, transcended mere topicality and presented certain universal and timeless themes that make an appeal in any age.

The war of the sexes, for example, is much the same whether the scene is the court of Queen Elizabeth I or the London of Queen Elizabeth II. Only the actors and the rules of the game change. Even the banalities of social raillery, the give-and-take of party repartee, follow recognizable patterns in the forests of the King of Navarre and across the cocktail glasses of café society. Men in all ages perhaps have jibed at women as the weaker vessels; and women have mocked when boastful men have fallen victims to feminine wiles. Insofar as *Love's Labor's Lost* has a plot, it revolves around the contest between the King of Navarre's little academy of studious men and the Princess of France's gay and coquettish ladies. But it is merely a make-believe contest because both the participants and the audience know that Navarre's cause is lost from the beginning. Shakespeare allows his audience to enjoy a prolonged jest at the expense of men vain enough to believe that they can resist temptations as old as Eve. Perhaps some event or situation gave this theme particular point for Shakespeare's audience; at this distance in time we cannot tell. Yet even without a topical focus the subject was universal and familiar enough to provide amusement for a willing audience.

It is always dangerous to read Shakespeare's own views into the words of any of his characters, but if we can imagine the author serving as chorus to his play, we might think of Berowne as the voice of Shakespeare's common sense. Berowne knows that the bookish affectations of the King and his courtiers will come to nought, and he is not impressed with the show of learning, which he deems pedantry. He knows that there is something more vital in life than merely repeating facts from books:

> Study is like the heaven's glorious sun,
> That will not be deep-searched with saucy looks;
> Small have continual plodders ever won,
> Save base authority from others' books.
> These earthly godfathers of heaven's lights,
> That give a name to every fixed star,
> Have no more profit of their shining nights
> Than those that walk and wot not what they are.
> Too much to know is to know nought but fame;
> And every godfather can give a name.

Though Berowne signs the compact to study three years without the solace of female company, he mocks the King's discomfiture at having to make an exception "on mere necessity" because of the immediate arrival of the Princess of France on a diplomatic mission:

> So study evermore is overshot.
> While it doth study to have what it would,
> It doth forget to do the thing it should;
> And when it hath the thing it hunteth most,
> 'Tis won as towns with fire—so won, so lost.

SOURCES AND BACKGROUND

Although we can be reasonably certain that Shakespeare used topical material and recognizable allusions in *Love's Labor's Lost*, the sources of this play have mystified scholars. If Shakespeare used an older play, it is unknown. If he used any tale, narrative, or history containing the plot elements of his play, they have escaped identification. No King of Navarre bore the name Ferdinand, but the name of Henry of Navarre, who became Henry IV of France, was much in the consciousness of Elizabethan Englishmen. The names of the followers of Shakespeare's King—Berowne, Longaville, and Dumaine—closely parallel the names of actual people in contemporary France. There is no question but that Shakespeare could have heard of them, since information about political affairs in France was readily available to Englishmen in numerous newsbooks and pamphlets. Among the surviving newsbooks are *A Caveat for France, upon the Present Evils That It Now Suffereth* (1588), *Credible Reports from France and Flanders in the Month of May, 1590* (1591), *The French History* (1589), *The True History of the Civil Wars in France* (1591), *An Excellent Discourse upon the Now Present Estate of France* (1592), and *The History of France* (1595). Such topical works were read not only by courtiers but by the average citizen of London, who was greatly concerned about events across the Channel that might affect not only religion and trade but also the peace of England. The Baron de Biron

(Berowne) and the Duke de Longueville were colleagues of Henry of Navarre, while Dumaine may recall an opponent of the King, Charles, Duke de Mayenne. The incident of the Princess' visit to Navarre may be based on an actual episode when Henry's estranged wife, Marguerite de Valois, visited him at Nérac in 1578 to discuss her dowry. Others have thought it refers to Catherine de Medici's visit to Henry at Saint Bris in 1586, at which time Queen Catherine tried to persuade Henry to divorce his dissolute wife, Marguerite, and marry Christine of Lorraine. That Shakespeare had this expedition in mind seems highly doubtful. A source for the idea of Henry's academy of ascetic scholars may have been Pierre de la Primaudaye's *The French Academy*, published in an English translation in 1586 and again in 1589, 1594, and several times thereafter. A popular encyclopedic work that Shakespeare might have known and used, it contains a passage describing the founding of an academy by four young men of Anjou. Though names of characters and a few episodes suggest some parallel to contemporary events, the fact remains that we cannot give any precise sources for this play.

If it was written for some special event, such as an entertainment of the Queen by one of her great nobles, the author would have sought the advice of the one who commissioned the play or his agent about desirable themes. It was customary for Elizabethan writers and dramatists to be commissioned to supply pageants, masks, and plays, written to order, for entertainments at court and elsewhere. It seems likely that someone familiar with recent events in France may have supplied Shakespeare with names and suggested the settings in Navarre.

English interest in Navarre had been acute. Indeed, Queen Elizabeth had given sporadic aid to Henry since 1589 in an effort to counter the influence of the Holy League. In January, 1591, Sir Roger Williams led an expeditionary force to Dieppe; in April of the same year, Sir John Norreys commanded a second contingent in France; and in July the Earl of Essex went over with English troops who joined Henry's army besieging Rouen. The siege of Rouen was raised in April, 1592, but still another contingent of English troops under the command of Norreys went to France in the summer of 1592.

All of this activity in support of Henry of Navarre kept English curiosity alive and made the utilization of a fictitious setting in Navarre a useful dramatic device. There is no reason to believe that Henry's espousal of the Catholic faith in 1593 suddenly wiped out popular interest in him and his court; many a realistic Englishman may have shared Henry's own view that Paris was worth a Mass. Certainly a vague setting at the court of Navarre, particularly a mildly satiric treatment, would have been palatable at any time in the 1590's.

Soldiers returning from France were full of talk about the expedition. The Earl of Essex's contingent had fought with the Marshal Biron's troops in front of Rouen, and Essex's officers admired Biron as a brave, gallant, and witty soldier, not unlike the character in Shakespeare's play. That Shakespeare picked up the French background for his play from some officer in the Essex expedition seems plausible.

Love's Labor's Lost, however, can hardly be called a play about an episode in French history. France merely supplied a shadowy background for a series of loosely connected scenes of entertainment more characteristic of the shows offered the Queen on her progresses than of the fully developed drama of the theatres. For these shows, Shakespeare drew on traditional material, both native and foreign. In the Italian *commedia dell' arte* stock characters like Holofernes, Armado, Moth, Costard, and the other comics had long been popular. Italian performers of *commedia dell' arte* are recorded in England as early as 1573, but long before this their particular type of comedy had become a part of the dramatic tradition of Western Europe. Although in *Love's Labor's Lost* Shakespeare uses these stock types, he manages as always to naturalize them and to give them an air of reality. If the rustics of *Love's Labor's Lost* with their show of the Nine Worthies cannot yet come up to the performance of the rude mechanicals in *Midsummer Night's Dream,* they nevertheless are beginning to emerge as something more than mere abstract types adapted from a foreign source.

The most popular writer of court comedies in the period of Shakespeare's apprenticeship was John Lyly, who achieved a reputation from his plays and his novel, *Euphues.* Although Shakespeare did not borrow extensively from Lyly, *Love's Labor's Lost* reflects something of the style of Lyly's characteristic comedies, particularly in the use of wordplay and fanciful phraseology, in some stock characters, and in the motif of courtly love. Lyly also was a master of allegory with topical applications. He knew just how far to go without offending, and just how much court gossip he might allude to without getting in the bad books of the authorities. We can imagine that the young Shakespeare took a leaf from this chapter in Lyly's book and, doubtless with the help of some experienced hand at court, managed to make his topical jests in safety.

If *Love's Labor's Lost* depended for its appeal merely upon its topical satire and its topical jokes, long since dead, it would not be worth our attention except as a fossil of Elizabethan courtly taste. Although the play contains many arid passages, it does reveal a poet of genius at work. Its poetic style is varied, as if the author were experimenting with many different forms. Written about the time of Shakespeare's sonnets and narrative poems, the play reveals the lyrical impulse characteristic of that period in the author's career. Although many passages merely reflect the poetic fashions of the sonneteering period, at times the author shows the originality and maturity of his later style. At one point he puts into Berowne's mouth a renunciation of literary fads and we can be sure that Shakespeare is speaking in his own voice:

> Taffeta phrases, silken terms precise,
> Three-piled hyperboles, spruce affectation,

Figures pedantical—these summer flies
Have blown me full of maggot ostentation.
I do forswear them; and I here protest,
By this white glove—how white the hand, God
  knows!—
Henceforth my wooing mind shall be expressed
In russet yeas, and honest kersey noes.
And, to begin, wench—so God help me, law!—
My love to thee is sound, sans crack or flaw.

Gone are the affectations of euphuism and of the fine writing characteristic of the sonneteers. Berowne and Shakespeare are no longer the slaves of fashion, and we can read the play with interest because of these touches of genuine lyric genius, culminating at the end in what one critic has declared to be one of the finest songs in the language.

Although much detail in the topical satire is now lost to us, and we merely pile pedantry upon pedantry in trying to explain every pun and all the verbal gymnastics of Holofernes and his brethren, yet on the stage even these scenes are not utterly lacking in humor. The mumbo jumbo, rendered by a skillful actor with the necessary stage business, is frequently funny, and here and there the common sense of some remark sheers through the pedantry and lets in a shaft of laughter. On the stage these characters are not wooden images but come to life in a way that the academic critic sometimes finds hard to comprehend.

DATE, TEXT, AND STAGE HISTORY

THE FIRST printed text of *Love's Labor's Lost* is the quarto of 1598, *A Pleasant Conceited Comedy Called Love's Labor's Lost. As it was presented before her Highness this last Christmas. Newly corrected and augmented. By W. Shakespeare.* The wording on the title page suggests that an earlier and perhaps corrupt version had been in print, but if so it appears to be irrevocably lost. The wording also indicates that the play was popular enough for a revival at court as part of the Christmas festivities in 1597. How much revision the play underwent for this performance is a matter of conjecture.

The date of the earliest performance is also the subject of much debate. From allusions to recent events in France, Professor H. B. Charlton decided that the original composition could be fixed at 1592. Sir Edmund Chambers, with his usual sound sense, declares: "So far as style is concerned, I see no evidence for two dates, and no evidence for a very early date. The versification is extremely adroit, and certainly not that of a beginner. I regard the play as the earliest of the lyrical group which includes *Midsummer Night's Dream, Romeo and Juliet,* and *Richard II,* and I put it in 1595." In the light of all the evidence, the year 1595 seems a reasonable date for composition and first performance.

The First Quarto of 1598, despite its claim of being "newly corrected," is full of printing errors, mislineation, and faulty punctuation. The First Folio of 1623 used for copy a corrected Quarto text, but the

Folio introduced many new errors. The present text is based on the First Quarto, with necessary corrections and emendations.

A Second Quarto was published in 1631, but it has no textual authority. Its title page described the play as "A witty and pleasant comedy, as it was acted by his Majesty's servants at the Blackfriars and the Globe," which suggests that it had considerable popularity in the playhouses in addition to its performance before the Queen. In 1605 the play was revived for a performance before James I's Queen, Anne of Denmark, as part of the festivities arranged at his house by the Earl of Southampton.

Love's Labor's Lost was not one of the plays that appealed to the Restoration, and indeed, it dropped out of favor for the next century and a half. In the nineteenth century it was occasionally played on both sides of the Atlantic, and it has had revivals from time to time in our generation. Since Shakespeare's own period, however, it has not been one of his most popular plays.

THE AUTHOR

As early as 1598 Shakespeare was so well known as a literary and dramatic craftsman that Francis Meres, in his *Palladis Tamia: Wits Treasury*, referred in flattering terms to him as "mellifluous and honey-tongued Shakespeare," famous for his *Venus and Adonis*, his *Lucrece*, and "his sugared sonnets," which were circulating "among his private friends." Meres observes further that "as Plautus and Seneca are accounted the best for comedy and tragedy among the Latins, so Shakespeare among the English is the most excellent in both kinds for the stage," and he mentions a dozen plays that had made a name for Shakespeare. He concludes with the remark "that the Muses would speak with Shakespeare's fine filed phrase if they would speak English."

To those acquainted with the history of the Elizabethan and Jacobean periods, it is incredible that anyone should be so naïve or ignorant as to doubt the reality of Shakespeare as the author of the plays that bear his name. Yet so much nonsense has been written about other "candidates" for the plays that it is well to remind readers that no credible evidence that would stand up in a court of law has ever been adduced to prove either that Shakespeare did not write his plays or that anyone else wrote them. All the theories offered for the authorship of Francis Bacon, the Earl of Derby, the Earl of Oxford, the Earl of Hertford, Christopher Marlowe, and a score of other candidates are mere conjectures spun from the active imaginations of persons who confuse hypothesis and conjecture with evidence.

As Meres' statement of 1598 indicates, Shakespeare was already a popular playwright whose name carried weight at the box office. The obvious reputation of Shakespeare as early as 1598 makes the effort to prove him a myth one of the most absurd in the history of human perversity.

The anti-Shakespeareans talk darkly about a plot

of vested interests to maintain the authorship of Shakespeare. Nobody has any vested interest in Shakespeare, but every scholar is interested in the truth and in the quality of evidence advanced by special pleaders who set forth hypotheses in place of facts.

The anti-Shakespeareans base their arguments upon a few simple premises, all of them false. These false premises are that Shakespeare was an unlettered yokel without any schooling, that nothing is known about Shakespeare, and that only a noble lord or the equivalent in background could have written the plays. The facts are that more is known about Shakespeare than about most dramatists of his day, that he had a very good education, acquired in the Stratford Grammar School, that the plays show no evidence of profound book learning, and that the knowledge of kings and courts evident in the plays is no greater than any intelligent young man could have picked up at second hand. Most anti-Shakespeareans are naïve and betray an obvious snobbery. The author of their favorite plays, they imply, must have had a college diploma framed and hung on his study wall like the one in their dentist's office, and obviously so great a writer must have had a title or some equally significant evidence of exalted social background. They forget that genius has a way of cropping up in unexpected places and that none of the great creative writers of the world got his inspiration in a college or university course.

William Shakespeare was the son of John Shakespeare of Stratford-upon-Avon, a substantial citizen of that small but busy market town in the center of the rich agricultural county of Warwick. John Shakespeare kept a shop, what we would call a general store; he dealt in wool and other produce and gradually acquired property. As a youth, John Shakespeare had learned the trade of glover and leather worker. There is no contemporary evidence that the elder Shakespeare was a butcher, though the anti-Shakespeareans like to talk about the ignorant "butcher's boy of Stratford." Their only evidence is a statement by gossipy John Aubrey, more than a century after William Shakespeare's birth, that young William followed his father's trade, and when he killed a calf, "he would do it in a high style and make a speech." We would like to believe the story true, but Aubrey is not a very credible witness.

John Shakespeare probably continued to operate a farm at Snitterfield that his father had leased. He married Mary Arden, daughter of his father's landlord, a man of some property. The third of their eight children was William, baptized on April 26, 1564, and probably born three days before. At least, it is conventional to celebrate April 23 as his birthday.

The Stratford records give considerable information about John Shakespeare. We know that he held several municipal offices including those of alderman and mayor. In 1580 he was in some sort of legal difficulty and was fined for neglecting a summons of the Court of Queen's Bench requiring him to appear at Westminster and be bound over to keep the peace.

As a citizen and alderman of Stratford, John Shakespeare was entitled to send his son to the grammar school free. Though the records are lost, there can be no reason to doubt that this is where young William received his education. As any student of the period knows, the grammar schools provided the basic education in Latin learning and literature. The Elizabethan grammar school is not to be confused with modern grammar schools. Many cultivated men of the day received all their formal education in the grammar schools. At the universities in this period a student would have received little training that would have inspired him to be a creative writer. At Stratford young Shakespeare would have acquired a familiarity with Latin and some little knowledge of Greek. He would have read Latin authors and become acquainted with the plays of Plautus and Terence. Undoubtedly, in this period of his life he received that stimulation to read and explore for himself the world of ancient and modern history which he later utilized in his plays. The youngster who does not acquire this type of intellectual curiosity *before* college days rarely develops as a result of a college course the kind of mind Shakespeare demonstrated. His learning in books was anything but profound, but he clearly had the probing curiosity that sent him in search of information, and he had a keenness in the observation of nature and of humankind that finds reflection in his poetry.

There is little documentation for Shakespeare's boyhood. There is little reason why there should be. Nobody knew that he was going to be a dramatist about whom any scrap of information would be prized in the centuries to come. He was merely an active and vigorous youth of Stratford, perhaps assisting his father in his business, and no Boswell bothered to write down facts about him. The most important record that we have is a marriage license issued by the Bishop of Worcester on November 28, 1582, to permit William Shakespeare to marry Anne Hathaway, seven or eight years his senior; furthermore, the Bishop permitted the marriage after reading the banns only once instead of three times, evidence of the desire for haste. The need was explained on May 26, 1583, when the christening of Susanna, daughter of William and Anne Shakespeare, was recorded at Stratford. Two years later, on February 2, 1585, the records show the birth of twins to the Shakespeares, a boy and a girl who were christened Hamnet and Judith.

What William Shakespeare was doing in Stratford during the early years of his married life, or when he went to London, we do not know. It has been conjectured that he tried his hand at schoolteaching, but that is a mere guess. There is a legend that he left Stratford to escape a charge of poaching in the park of Sir Thomas Lucy of Charlecote, but there is no proof of this. There is also a legend that when first he came to London, he earned his living by holding horses outside a playhouse and presently was given employment inside, but there is nothing better than eighteenth-century hearsay for this. How Shakespeare broke into the London theatres as a dramatist and actor we do not know. But lack of information is not surprising, for Elizabethans did not write their autobiographies, and we know even less about the lives of many writers and some men of affairs than we know about Shakespeare. By 1592 he was so well established and popular that he incurred the envy of the dramatist and pamphleteer Robert Greene, who referred to him as an "upstart crow . . . in his own conceit the only Shake-scene in a country." From this time onward, contemporary allusions and references in legal documents enable the scholar to chart Shakespeare's career with greater accuracy than is possible with most other Elizabethan dramatists.

By 1594 Shakespeare was a member of the company of actors known as the Lord Chamberlain's Men. After the accession of James I, in 1603, the company would have the sovereign for their patron and would be known as the King's Men. During the period of its greatest prosperity, this company would have as its principal theatres the Globe and the Blackfriars. Shakespeare was both an actor and a shareholder in the company. Tradition has assigned him such acting roles as Adam in *As You Like It* and the Ghost in *Hamlet*, a modest place on the stage that suggests that he may have had other duties in the management of the company. Such conclusions, however, are based on surmise.

What we do know is that his plays were popular

and that he was highly successful in his vocation. His first play may have been *The Comedy of Errors,* acted perhaps in 1591. Certainly this was one of his earliest plays. The three parts of *Henry VI* were acted sometime between 1590 and 1592. Critics are not in agreement about precisely how much Shakespeare wrote of these three plays. *Richard III* probably dates from 1593. With this play Shakespeare captured the imagination of Elizabethan audiences, then enormously interested in historical plays. With *Richard III* Shakespeare also gave an interpretation pleasing to the Tudors of the rise to power of the grandfather of Queen Elizabeth. From this time onward, Shakespeare's plays followed on the stage in rapid succession: *Titus Andronicus, The Taming of the Shrew, The Two Gentlemen of Verona, Love's Labor's Lost, Romeo and Juliet, Richard II, A Midsummer Night's Dream, King John, The Merchant of Venice, Henry IV (Parts 1 and 2), Much Ado About Nothing, Henry V, Julius Cæsar, As You Like It, Twelfth Night, Hamlet, The Merry Wives of Windsor, All's Well That Ends Well, Measure for Measure, Othello, King Lear,* and nine others that followed before Shakespeare retired completely, about 1613.

In the course of his career in London, he made enough money to enable him to retire to Stratford with a competence. His purchase on May 4, 1597, of New Place, then the second-largest dwelling in Stratford, a "pretty house of brick and timber," with a handsome garden, indicates his increasing prosperity. There his wife and children lived while he busied himself in the London theatres. The summer before he acquired New Place, his life was darkened by the death of his only son, Hamnet, a child of eleven. In May, 1602, Shakespeare purchased one hundred and seven acres of fertile farmland near Stratford and a few months later bought a cottage and garden across the alley from New Place. About 1611, he seems to have returned permanently to Stratford, for the next year a legal document refers to him as "William Shakespeare of Stratford-upon-Avon . . . gentleman." To achieve the desired appellation of gentleman, William Shakespeare had seen to it that the College of Heralds in 1596 granted his father a coat of arms. In one step he thus became a second-generation gentleman.

Shakespeare's daughter Susanna made a good match in 1607 with Dr. John Hall, a prominent and prosperous Stratford physician. His second daughter, Judith, did not marry until she was thirty-two years old, and then, under somewhat scandalous circumstances, she married Thomas Quiney, a Stratford vintner. On March 25, 1616, Shakespeare made his will, bequeathing his landed property to Susanna, £300 to Judith, certain sums to other relatives, and his second-best bed to his wife, Anne. Much has been made of the second-best bed, but the legacy probably indicates only that Anne liked that particular bed. Shakespeare, following the practice of the time, may have already arranged with Susanna for his wife's care. Finally, on April 23, 1616, the anniversary of his birth, William Shakespeare died, and he was buried on April 25 within the chancel of Trinity Church, as befitted an honored citizen. On August 6, 1623, a few months before the publication of the collected edition of Shakespeare's plays, Anne Shakespeare joined her husband in death.

THE PUBLICATION OF HIS PLAYS

During his lifetime Shakespeare made no effort to publish any of his plays, though eighteen appeared in print in single-play editions known as quartos. Some of these are corrupt versions known as "bad quartos." No quarto, so far as is known, had the author's approval. Plays were not considered "literature" any more than most radio and television scripts today are considered literature. Dramatists sold their plays outright to the theatrical companies and it was usually considered in the company's interest to keep plays from getting into print. To achieve a reputation as a man of letters, Shakespeare wrote his *Sonnets* and his narrative poems, *Venus and Adonis* and *The Rape of Lucrece*, but he probably never dreamed that his plays would establish his reputation as a literary genius. Only Ben Jonson, a man known for his colossal conceit, had the crust to call his plays *Works*, as he did when he published an edition in 1616. But men laughed at Ben Jonson.

After Shakespeare's death, two of his old colleagues in the King's Men, John Heminges and Henry Condell, decided that it would be a good thing to print, in more accurate versions than were then available, the plays already published and eighteen additional plays not previously published in quarto. In 1623 appeared *Mr. William Shakespeares Comedies, Histories, & Tragedies. Published according to the True Originall Copies. London. Printed by Isaac Iaggard and Ed. Blount.* This was the famous First Folio, a work that had the authority of Shakespeare's associates. The only play commonly attributed to Shakespeare that was omitted in the First Folio was *Pericles*. In their preface, "To the great Variety of Readers," Heminges and Condell state that whereas "you were abused with diverse stolen and surreptitious copies, maimed and deformed by the frauds and stealths of injurious impostors that exposed them, even those are now offered to your view cured and perfect of their limbs; and all the rest, absolute in their numbers, as he conceived them." What they used for printer's copy is one of the vexed problems of scholarship, and skilled bibliographers have devoted years of study to the question of the relation of the "copy" for the First Folio to Shakespeare's manuscripts. In some cases it is clear that the editors corrected printed quarto versions of the plays, probably by comparison with playhouse scripts. Whether these scripts were in Shakespeare's autograph is anybody's guess. No manuscript of any play in Shakespeare's handwriting has survived. Indeed, very few play manuscripts from this period by any author are extant. The Tudor and Stuart periods had not yet learned to prize autographs and authors' original manuscripts.

Since the First Folio contains eighteen plays not previously printed, it is the only source for these. For the other eighteen, which had appeared in quarto versions, the First Folio also has the authority of an edition prepared and overseen by Shakespeare's colleagues and professional associates. But since editorial standards in 1623 were far from strict, and Heminges and Condell were actors rather than editors by profession, the texts are sometimes careless. The printing and proofreading of the First Folio also left much to be desired, and some garbled passages have had to be corrected and emended. The "good quarto" texts have to be taken into account in preparing a modern edition.

Because of the great popularity of Shakespeare through the centuries, the First Folio has become a prized book, but it is not a very rare one, for it is estimated that 238 copies are extant. The Folger Shakespeare Library in Washington, D.C., has seventy-nine copies of the First Folio, collected by the founder, Henry Clay Folger, who believed that a collation of as many texts as possible would reveal significant facts about the text of Shakespeare's plays. Dr. Charlton Hinman, using an ingenious machine of his own invention for mechanical collating, has made many discoveries that throw light on Shakespeare's text and on printing practices of the day.

The probability is that the First Folio of 1623 had an edition of between 1,000 and 1,250 copies. It is believed that it sold for £1, which made it an expensive book, for £1 in 1623 was equivalent to something between $40 and $50 in modern purchasing power.

During the seventeenth century, Shakespeare was sufficiently popular to warrant three later editions in folio size, the Second Folio of 1632, the Third Folio of 1663–1664, and the Fourth Folio of 1685. The Third Folio added six other plays ascribed to Shakespeare, but these are apocryphal.

THE SHAKESPEAREAN THEATRE

The theatres in which Shakespeare's plays were performed were vastly different from those we know today. The stage was a platform that jutted out into the area now occupied by the first rows of seats on the main floor, what is called the "orchestra" in America and the "pit" in England. This platform had no curtain to come down at the ends of acts and scenes. And although simple stage properties were available, the Elizabethan theatre lacked both the machinery and the elaborate movable scenery of the modern theatre. In the rear of the platform stage was a curtained area that could be used as an inner room, a tomb, or any such scene that might be required. A balcony above this inner room, and perhaps balconies on the sides of the stage, could represent the upper deck of a ship, the entry to Juliet's room, or a prison window. A trap door in the stage provided an entrance for ghosts and devils from the nether regions, and a similar trap in the canopied structure over the stage, known as the "heavens," made it possible to let down angels on a rope. These primitive stage arrangements help to account for many elements in Elizabethan plays. For example, since there was no curtain, the dramatist frequently felt the necessity of writing into his play action to clear the stage at the ends of acts and scenes. The funeral march at the end of *Hamlet* is not there merely for atmosphere; Shakespeare had to get the corpses off the stage. The lack of scenery also freed the dramatist from undue concern about the exact location of his sets, and the physical relation of his various settings to each other did not have to be worked out with the same precision as in the modern theatre.

Before London had buildings designed exclusively for theatrical entertainment, plays were given in inns and taverns. The characteristic inn of the period had an inner courtyard with rooms opening onto balconies overlooking the yard. Players could set up their temporary stages at one end of the yard and audiences could find seats on the balconies out of the weather. The poorer sort could stand or sit on the cobblestones in the yard, which was open to the sky. The first theatres followed this construction, and throughout the Elizabethan period the large public theatres had a yard in front of the stage open to the weather, with two or three tiers of covered balconies extending around the theatre. This physical structure again influenced the writing of plays. Because a dramatist wanted the actors to be heard, he frequently wrote into his play orations that could be delivered with declamatory effect. He also provided spectacle, buffoonery, and broad jests to keep the riotous groundlings in the yard entertained and quiet.

In another respect the Elizabethan theatre differed greatly from ours. It had no actresses. All women's roles were taken by boys, sometimes recruited from the boys' choirs of the London churches. Some of these youths acted their roles with great skill and the Elizabethans did not seem to be aware of any incongruity. The first actresses on the professional English stage appeared after the Restoration of Charles II, in 1660, when exiled Englishmen brought back from France practices of the French stage.

London in the Elizabethan period, as now, was the center of theatrical interest, though wandering actors from time to time traveled through the country performing in inns, halls, and the houses of the nobility. The first professional playhouse, called simply The Theatre, was erected by James Burbage, father of Shakespeare's colleague Richard Burbage, in 1576 on lands of the old Holywell Priory adjacent to Finsbury Fields, a playground and park area just north of the city walls. It had the advantage of being outside the city's jurisdiction and yet was near enough to be easily accessible. Soon after The Theatre was opened, another playhouse called The Curtain was erected in the same neighborhood. Both of these playhouses had open courtyards and were probably polygonal in shape.

About the time The Curtain opened, Richard Farrant, Master of the Children of the Chapel Royal at Windsor and of St. Paul's, conceived the idea of opening a "private" theatre in the old monastery buildings of the Blackfriars, not far from St. Paul's Cathedral in the heart of the city. This theatre was ostensibly to train the choirboys in plays for presentation at Court, but Farrant managed to present plays to paying audiences and achieved considerable success until aristocratic neighbors complained and had the theatre closed. This first Blackfriars Theatre was significant, however, because it popularized the boy actors in a professional way and it paved the way for a second theatre in the Blackfriars, which Shakespeare's company took over more than thirty years later. By the last years of the sixteenth century, London had at least six professional theatres and still others were erected during the reign of James I.

The Globe Theatre, the playhouse that most people connect with Shakespeare, was erected early in 1599 on the Bankside, the area across the Thames from the city. Its construction had a dramatic beginning, for on the night of December 28, 1598, James Burbage's sons, Cuthbert and Richard, gathered together a crew who tore down the old theatre in Holywell and carted the timbers across the river to a site that they had chosen for a new playhouse. The reason for this clandestine operation was a row with the landowner over the lease to the Holywell property. The site chosen for the Globe was another playground outside of the city's jurisdiction, a region of somewhat unsavory character. Not far away was the Bear Garden, an amphitheatre devoted to the baiting of bears and bulls.

This was also the region occupied by many houses of ill fame licensed by the Bishop of Winchester and the source of substantial revenue to him. But it was easily accessible either from London Bridge or by means of the cheap boats operated by the London watermen, and it had the great advantage of being beyond the authority of the Puritanical aldermen of London, who frowned on plays because they lured apprentices from work, filled their heads with improper ideas, and generally exerted a bad influence. The aldermen also complained that the crowds drawn together in the theatre helped to spread the plague.

The Globe was the handsomest theatre up to its time. It was a large building, apparently octagonal in shape and open like its predecessors to the sky in the center, but capable of seating a large audience in its covered balconies. To erect and operate the Globe, the Burbages organized a syndicate composed of the leading members of the dramatic company, of which Shakespeare was a member. Since it was open to the weather and depended on natural light, plays had to be given in the afternoon. This caused no hardship in the long afternoons of an English summer, but in the winter the weather was a great handicap and discouraged all except the hardiest. For that reason, in 1608 Shakespeare's company was glad to take over the lease of the second Blackfriars Theatre, a substantial, roomy hall reconstructed within the framework of the old monastery building. This theatre was protected from the weather and its stage was artificially lighted by chandeliers of candles. This became the winter playhouse for Shakespeare's company and at once proved so popular that the congestion of traffic created an embarrassing problem. Stringent regulations had to be made for the movement of coaches in the vicinity. Shakespeare's company continued to use the Globe during the summer months. In 1613 a squib fired from a cannon during a performance of *Henry VIII* fell on the thatched roof and the Globe burned to the ground. The next year it was rebuilt.

London had other famous theatres. The Rose, just west of the Globe, was built by Philip Henslowe, a semiliterate denizen of the Bankside, who became one of the most important theatrical owners and producers of the Tudor and Stuart periods. What is more important for historians, he kept a detailed account book, which provides much of our information about theatrical history in his time. Another famous theatre on the Bankside was the Swan, which a Dutch priest, Johannes de Witt, visited in 1596. The crude drawing of the stage which he made was copied by his friend Arend van Buchell; it is one of the important pieces of contemporary evidence for theatrical construction. Among the other theatres, the Fortune, north of the city, on Golding Lane, and the Red Bull, even farther away from the city, off St. John's Street, were the most popular. The Red Bull, much frequented by apprentices, favored sensational and sometimes rowdy plays.

The actors who kept all of these theatres going

were organized into companies under the protection of some noble patron. Traditionally actors had enjoyed a low reputation. In some of the ordinances they were classed as vagrants; in the phraseology of the time, "rogues, vagabonds, sturdy beggars, and common players" were all listed together as undesirables. To escape penalties often meted out to these characters, organized groups of actors managed to gain the protection of various personages of high degree. In the later years of Elizabeth's reign, a group flourished under the name of the Queen's Men; another group had the protection of the Lord Admiral and were known as the Lord Admiral's Men. Edward Alleyn, son-in-law of Philip Henslowe, was the leading spirit in the Lord Admiral's Men. Besides the adult companies, troupes of boy actors from time to time also enjoyed considerable popularity. Among these were the Children of Paul's and the Children of the Chapel Royal.

The company with which Shakespeare had a long association had for its first patron Henry Carey, Lord Hunsdon, the Lord Chamberlain, and hence they were known as the Lord Chamberlain's Men. After the accession of James I, they became the King's Men. This company was the great rival of the Lord Admiral's Men, managed by Henslowe and Alleyn.

All was not easy for the players in Shakespeare's time, for the aldermen of London were always eager for an excuse to close up the Blackfriars and any other theatres in their jurisdiction. The theatres outside the jurisdiction of London were not immune from interference, for they might be shut up by order of the Privy Council for meddling in politics or for various other offenses, or they might be closed in time of plague lest they spread infection. During plague times, the actors usually went on tour and played the provinces wherever they could find an audience. Particularly frightening were the plagues of 1592–1594 and 1613 when the theatres closed and the players, like many other Londoners, had to take to the country.

Though players had a low social status, they enjoyed great popularity, and one of the favorite forms of entertainment at court was the performance of plays. To be commanded to perform at court conferred great prestige upon a company of players, and printers frequently noted that fact when they published plays. Several of Shakespeare's plays were performed before the sovereign, and Shakespeare himself undoubtedly acted in some of these plays.

REFERENCES FOR FURTHER READING

MANY READERS will want suggestions for further reading about Shakespeare and his times. The literature in this field is enormous but a few references will serve as guides to further study. A simple and useful little book is Gerald Sanders, *A Shakespeare Primer* (New York, 1950). *A Companion to Shakespeare Studies*, edited by Harley Granville-Barker and G. B. Harrison (Cambridge, 1934) is a valuable guide. More detailed but still not so voluminous as to be confusing is Hazelton Spencer, *The Art and Life of William Shakespeare* (New York, 1940) which, like Sanders' handbook, contains a brief annotated list of useful books on various aspects of the subject. The most detailed and scholarly work providing complete factual information about Shakespeare is Sir Edmund Chambers, *William Shakespeare: A Study of Facts and Problems* (2 vols., Oxford, 1930). For detailed, factual information about the Elizabethan and seventeenth-century stages, the definitive reference works are Sir Edmund Chambers, *The Elizabethan Stage* (4 vols., Oxford, 1923) and Gerald E. Bentley, *The Jacobean and Caroline Stage* (5 vols., Oxford, 1941–1956). Alfred Harbage, *Shakespeare's Audience* (New York, 1941) throws light on the nature and tastes of the customers for whom Elizabethan dramatists wrote.

Although specialists disagree about details of stage construction, the reader will find essential information in John C. Adams, *The Globe Playhouse: Its Design and Equipment* (Barnes & Noble, 1961). A model of the Globe playhouse by Dr. Adams is on permanent exhibition in the Folger Shakespeare Library in Washington, D.C. An excellent description of the architecture of the Globe is Irwin Smith, *Shakespeare's Globe Playhouse: A Modern Reconstruction in Text and Scale Drawings Based upon the Reconstruction of the Globe by John Cranford Adams* (New York, 1956). Another recent study of the physical characteristics of the

Globe is C. Walter Hodges, *The Globe Restored* (London, 1953). An easily read history of the early theatres is J. Q. Adams, *Shakespearean Playhouses: A History of English Theatres from the Beginnings to the Restoration* (Boston, 1917).

The following titles on theatrical history will provide information about Shakespeare's plays in later periods: Alfred Harbage, *Theatre for Shakespeare* (Toronto, 1955); Esther Cloudman Dunn, *Shakespeare in America* (New York, 1939); George C. D. Odell, *Shakespeare from Betterton to Irving* (2 vols., London, 1931); Arthur Colby Sprague, *Shakespeare and the Actors: The Stage Business in His Plays (1660–1905)* (Cambridge, Mass., 1944) and *Shakespearian Players and Performances* (Cambridge, Mass., 1953); Leslie Hotson, *The Commonwealth and Restoration Stage* (Cambridge, Mass., 1928); Alwin Thaler, *Shakspere to Sheridan: A Book About the Theatre of Yesterday and To-day* (Cambridge, Mass., 1922); Ernest Bradlee Watson, *Sheridan to Robertson: A Study of the 19th-Century London Stage* (Cambridge, Mass., 1926). Enid Welsford, *The Court Masque* (Cambridge, Mass., 1927) is an excellent study of the characteristics of this form of entertainment.

Harley Granville-Barker, *Prefaces to Shakespeare* (5 vols., London, 1927–1948) provides stimulating critical discussion of the plays. An older classic of criticism is Andrew C. Bradley, *Shakespearean Tragedy: Lectures on Hamlet, Othello, King Lear, Macbeth* (London, 1904), which is now available in an inexpensive reprint (New York, 1955). Thomas

M. Parrot, *Shakespearean Comedy* (New York, 1949) is scholarly and readable. Shakespeare's dramatizations of English history are examined in E. M. W. Tillyard, *Shakespeare's History Plays* (London, 1948), and Lily Bess Campbell, *Shakespeare's "Histories," Mirrors of Elizabethan Policy* (San Marino, Calif., 1947) contains a more technical discussion of the same subject.

Love's Labor's Lost has accumulated a considerable literature, some of it now much outdated. An exceptionally able study, even if one does not accept the dating that he proposes, is H. B. Charlton, "The Date of *Love's Labor's Lost,*" *The Modern Language Review*, XIII (1918), 257–266, 387–400. Professor Charlton summarizes a great deal of the previous scholarship concerned with the historical allusions and supposed sources of the play. Another excellent study describing the relation of the play to Italian comedy, especially to the *commedia dell' arte,* is O. J. Campbell, "*Love's Labor's Lost* Re-Studied," in *Studies in Shakespeare, Milton and Donne.* University of Michigan Publications (New York, 1925), pp. 1–46. Up-to-date and informative is W. Schrickx, *Shakespeare's Early Contemporaries: The Background of the Harvey-Nashe Polemic and Love's Labor's Lost* (Antwerp, 1956). Harley Granville-Barker, *Prefaces to Shakespeare,* Vol. II (London, 1958) has the most sensible comment on the staging and theatrical impact of this play. Possible identification of characters in *Love's Labor's Lost* with Elizabethan personalities is discussed in Frances Yates, *A Study of Love's Labor's Lost* (Cambridge,

1936). Some scholars have thought that Shakespeare refers to Raleigh and his circle in the "school of night" reference (Act IV. Sc. iii, l. 271), but this view is refuted by Ernest A. Strathmann, *Sir Walter Ralegh: A Study in Elizabethan Skepticism* (New York, 1951), pp. 262–271. Mr. Strathmann's book provides further references to the literature on this subject.

The question of the authenticity of Shakespeare's plays arouses perennial attention. A book that demolishes the notion of hidden cryptograms in the plays is William F. Friedman and Elizebeth S. Friedman, *The Shakespearean Ciphers Examined* (New York, 1957). A succinct account of the various absurdities advanced to suggest the authorship of a multitude of candidates other than Shakespeare will be found in R. C. Churchill's *Shakespeare and His Betters* (Bloomington, Ind., 1959) and Frank W. Wadsworth, *The Poacher from Stratford: A Partial Account of the Controversy over the Authorship of Shakespeare's Plays* (Berkeley, Calif., 1958). An essay on the curious notions in the writings of the anti-Shakespeareans is that by Louis B. Wright, "The Anti-Shakespeare Industry and the Growth of Cults," *The Virginia Quarterly Review*, XXXV (1959), 289–303.

Reprints of some of the sources of Shakespeare's plays can be found in *Shakespeare's Library* (2 vols., 1850), edited by John Payne Collier, and *The Shakespeare Classics* (12 vols., 1907–1926), edited by Israel Gollancz. Geoffrey Bullough, *Narrative and Dramatic Sources of Shakespeare* is a new series of volumes reprinting the sources. Three volumes covering the early comedies, comedies (1597–1603), and histories are now available. For discussion of Shakespeare's use of his sources see Kenneth Muir, *Shakespeare's Sources: Comedies and Tragedies* (London, 1957). Thomas M. Cranfill has recently edited a facsimile reprint of *Riche His Farewell to Military Profession* (1581), which contains stories that Shakespeare probably used for several of his plays.

Interesting pictures as well as new information about Shakespeare will be found in F. E. Halliday, *Shakespeare, a Pictorial Biography* (London, 1956). Allardyce Nicoll, *The Elizabethans* (Cambridge, 1957) contains a variety of illustrations.

A brief, clear, and accurate account of Tudor history is S. T. Bindoff, *The Tudors*, in the Penguin series. A readable general history is G. M. Trevelyan, *The History of England*, first published in 1926 and available in many editions. G. M. Trevelyan, *English Social History*, first published in 1942 and also available in many editions, provides fascinating information about England in all periods. Sir John Neale, *Queen Elizabeth* (London, 1934) is the best study of the great Queen. Various aspects of life in the Elizabethan period are treated in Louis B. Wright, *Middle-Class Culture in Elizabethan England* (Chapel Hill, N.C., 1935); reprinted by Cornell University Press, 1958). *Shakespeare's England: An Account of the Life and Manners of His Age*, edited by Sidney Lee and C. T. Onions (2 vols., Oxford, 1916), provides a large amount of information on many aspects of life in the Elizabethan period. Additional information will be found in Muriel St. C. Byrne, *Elizabethan Life in Town and Country* (Barnes & Noble, 1961).

The Folger Shakespeare Library is currently publishing a series of illustrated pamphlets on various aspects of English life in the sixteenth and seventeenth centuries. The following titles are available: Dorothy E. Mason, *Music in Elizabethan England;* Craig R. Thompson, *The English Church in the Sixteenth Century;* Louis B. Wright, *Shakespeare's Theatre and the Dramatic Tradition;* Giles E. Dawson, *The Life of William Shakespeare;* Virginia A. LaMar, *English Dress in the Age of Shakespeare;* Craig R. Thompson, *The Bible in English, 1525–1611;* Craig R. Thompson, *Schools in Tudor England;* Craig R. Thompson, *Universities in Tudor England;* Lilly C. Stone, *English Sports and Recreations;* Conyers Read, *The Government of England under Elizabeth;* Virginia A. LaMar, *Travel and Roads in England;* John R. Hale, *The Art of War and Rennaissance England;* and Albert J. Schmidt, *The Yeoman in Tudor and Stuart England.*

[*Dramatis Personae*

Ferdinand, King of Navarre.
Berowne, *Longaville,* *Dumaine,* } lords attending the King.
Boyet, *Marcade,* } lords attending the *Princess of France.*
Don Adriano de Armado, a fantastical Spaniard.
Sir Nathaniel, a curate.
Holofernes, a schoolmaster.
Anthony Dull, a constable.
Costard, a clown.
Moth, page to *Armado.*
A Forester.

The Princess of France.
Rosaline, *Maria,* *Katharine,* } ladies attending the *Princess.*
Jaquenetta, a country wench.

Lords, Attendants, etc.

SCENE: *The King of Navarre's Park*]

LOVE'S LABOR'S LOST

ACT I

I.[i.] The King of Navarre and the Lords Longaville, Berowne, and Dumaine have vowed to spend their time in study for three years, renouncing the company of women for that period. Berowne protests the absurdity of this but agrees to sign the vow. Immediately the King is faced with the necessity of relaxing the rule against women because of the imminent visit of the Princess of France on a diplomatic mission. In the meantime, the rustic Costard has been taken in the company of Jaquenetta and arrested for breaking the new law against consorting with women. The King assigns him to the custody of Armado, a fantastic Spaniard.

3. **grace:** honor; **disgrace:** misfortune.

4. **cormorant:** insatiable.

6. **bate:** blunt.

9. **affections:** inclinations of all kinds, not solely referring to amorous affections.

13. **academe:** a school after the Platonic model.

14. **living art:** the art of perfect living.

Time. From Jean de Serres, *A General Inventory of the History of France* (1611)

ACT I

[Scene I. The King of Navarre's Park.]

Enter Ferdinand, King of Navarre, Berowne, Longaville, and Dumaine.

King. Let fame, that all hunt after in their lives,
Live regist'red upon our brazen tombs,
And then grace us in the disgrace of death;
When, spite of cormorant devouring Time,
The endeavor of this present breath may buy 5
That honor which shall bate his scythe's keen edge,
And make us heirs of all eternity.
Therefore, brave conquerors—for so you are,
That war against your own affections
And the huge army of the world's desires— 10
Our late edict shall strongly stand in force:
Navarre shall be the wonder of the world;
Our court shall be a little academe,
Still and contemplative in living art.
You three, Berowne, Dumaine, and Longaville, 15
Have sworn for three years' term to live with me
My fellow scholars, and to keep those statutes
That are recorded in this schedule here.
Your oaths are passed; and now subscribe your names, 20

22. **branch:** division; portion.

24. **deep:** of profound import.

27. **Fat paunches have lean pates:** a proverbial idea. **Pates** equals "heads" (brains).

29. **mortified:** insensible to worldly temptations.

33. **With all these living in philosophy:** since all these (love, wealth, pomp) are to be found in philosophy.

51. **an if:** if.

The King of France. From Cesare Vecellio, *Habiti antichi et moderni di tutto il mondo* (1598)

That his own hand may strike his honor down
That violates the smallest branch herein:
If you are armed to do as sworn to do,
Subscribe to your deep oaths, and keep it too.
Long. I am resolved; 'tis but a three years' fast: 25
The mind shall banquet, though the body pine.
Fat paunches have lean pates; and dainty bits
Make rich the ribs, but bankrupt quite the wits.
Dum. My loving lord, Dumaine is mortified.
The grosser manner of these world's delights 30
He throws upon the gross world's baser slaves;
To love, to wealth, to pomp, I pine and die,
With all these living in philosophy.
Ber. I can but say their protestation over;
So much, dear liege, I have already sworn, 35
That is, to live and study here three years.
But there are other strict observances,
As: not to see a woman in that term,
Which I hope well is not enrolled there;
And one day in a week to touch no food, 40
And but one meal on every day beside,
The which I hope is not enrolled there;
And then to sleep but three hours in the night
And not be seen to wink of all the day—
When I was wont to think no harm all night, 45
And make a dark night too of half the day—
Which I hope well is not enrolled there.
O, these are barren tasks, too hard to keep,
Not to see ladies, study, fast, not sleep!
King. Your oath is passed to pass away from these. 50
Ber. Let me say no, my liege, an if you please:

60. **common sense:** i.e., everyone's knowledge or sight.

69. **troth:** faith.

70-1. **If study's gain be thus, and this be so,/ Study knows that which yet it doth not know:** if I thus achieve only skill in cheating, I will not have attained the true end of study, the discovery of truth.

74. **train:** entice.

76. **purchased:** acquired.

80. **Light, seeking light, doth light of light beguile:** the act of seeking the light of truth by the light of vision results in loss of sight. **Beguile** means cheat.

I only swore to study with your Grace,
And stay here in your court for three years' space.
Long. You swore to that, Berowne, and to the rest.
Ber. By yea and nay, sir, then I swore in jest. 55
What is the end of study, let me know.
King. Why, that to know which else we should not know.
Ber. Things hid and barred, you mean, from common sense? 60
King. Ay, that is study's godlike recompense.
Ber. Come on, then; I will swear to study so,
To know the thing I am forbid to know,
As thus: to study where I well may dine,
When I to feast expressly am forbid; 65
Or study where to meet some mistress fine,
When mistresses from common sense are hid;
Or, having sworn too hard-a-keeping oath,
Study to break it, and not break my troth.
If study's gain be thus, and this be so, 70
Study knows that which yet it doth not know.
Swear me to this, and I will ne'er say no.
King. These be the stops that hinder study quite,
And train our intellects to vain delight.
Ber. Why, all delights are vain, but that most vain 75
Which, with pain purchased, doth inherit pain:
As painfully to pore upon a book
To seek the light of truth; while truth the while
Doth falsely blind the eyesight of his look.
Light, seeking light, doth light of light beguile; 80
So, ere you find where light in darkness lies,
Your light grows dark by losing of your eyes.

83. **Study me:** let me study.

85. **Who dazzling so:** i.e., the eye, being dazzled by the sight of the **fairer eye; his heed:** the only thing that he heeds.

94. **wot:** know.

95. **Too much to know is to know nought but fame:** book learning consists only in knowing what others have advertised as the truth.

102. **green geese:** goslings; also, simpletons.

108. **envious:** malicious; **sneaping:** nipping.

109. **first-born infants:** earliest buds.

111. **boast:** vaunt itself.

Study me how to please the eye indeed,
By fixing it upon a fairer eye;
Who dazzling so, that eye shall be his heed, 85
And give him light that it was blinded by.
Study is like the heaven's glorious sun,
That will not be deep-searched with saucy looks;
Small have continual plodders ever won,
Save base authority from others' books. 90
These earthly godfathers of heaven's lights,
That give a name to every fixed star,
Have no more profit of their shining nights
Than those that walk and wot not what they are.
Too much to know is to know nought but fame; 95
And every godfather can give a name.

King. How well he's read, to reason against reading!

Dum. Proceeded well, to stop all good proceeding!

Long. He weeds the corn, and still lets grow the weeding. 100

Ber. The spring is near, when green geese are a-breeding.

Dum. How follows that?

Ber. Fit in his place and time. 105

Dum. In reason nothing.

Ber. Something then in rhyme.

Long. Berowne is like an envious sneaping frost
That bites the first-born infants of the spring.

Ber. Well, say I am; why should proud summer boast 110
Before the birds have any cause to sing?
Why should I joy in an abortive birth?

124. **Yet confident:** ever faithful.

125. **bide:** endure; **each three years' day:** each day of the three-year period.

136. **Marry:** indeed.

140. **gentility:** gentle behavior; i.e., the civilizing influence of women would be lost as a result of such a law.

Arman de Biron.

From *Chronologie et sommaire des souverains, pontifes, anciens péres* (1622)

At Christmas I no more desire a rose
Than wish a snow in May's newfangled shows;
But like of each thing that in season grows;
So you, to study now it is too late,
Climb o'er the house to unlock the little gate.

King. Well, sit you out; go home, Berowne; adieu.

Ber. No, my good lord; I have sworn to stay with you;
And though I have for barbarism spoke more
Than for that angel knowledge you can say,
Yet confident I'll keep what I have swore,
And bide the penance of each three years' day.
Give me the paper; let me read the same;
And to the strictest decrees I'll write my name.

King. How well this yielding rescues thee from shame!

Ber. [*Reads*] "Item. That no woman shall come within a mile of my court"—Hath this been proclaimed?

Long. Four days ago.

Ber. Let's see the penalty. [*Reads*] "—on pain of losing her tongue." Who devised this penalty?

Long. Marry, that did I.

Ber. Sweet lord, and why?

Long. To fright them hence with that dread penalty.

Ber. A dangerous law against gentility!
[*Reads*] "Item. If any man be seen to talk with a woman within the term of three years, he shall endure such public shame as the rest of the court can possibly devise."

155. **overshot:** defeated.

159. **won as towns with fire:** gained by means which defeat the end, like the taking of a town which has been destroyed by the fires of the besieging forces.

164. **affects:** natural tendencies.

168. **at large:** in full.

170. **in attainder of:** condemned to.

171. **Suggestions:** temptations.

174. **quick:** lively.

This article, my liege, yourself must break; 14
For well you know here comes in embassy
The French king's daughter, with yourself to speak—
A maid of grace and complete majesty—
About surrender up of Aquitaine
To her decrepit, sick, and bedrid father; 15
Therefore this article is made in vain,
Or vainly comes the admired princess hither.
King. What say you, lords? Why, this was quite forgot.
Ber. So study evermore is overshot. 15
While it doth study to have what it would,
It doth forget to do the thing it should;
And when it hath the thing it hunteth most,
'Tis won as towns with fire—so won, so lost.
King. We must of force dispense with this decree; 16
She must lie here on mere necessity.
Ber. Necessity will make us all forsworn
Three thousand times within this three years' space;
For every man with his affects is born,
Not by might mast'red, but by special grace. 16
If I break faith, this word shall speak for me:
I am forsworn on mere necessity.
So to the laws at large I write my name, [*Subscribes*]
And he that breaks them in the least degree
Stands in attainder of eternal shame. 17
Suggestions are to other as to me;
But I believe, although I seem so loath,
I am the last that will last keep his oath.
But is there no quick recreation granted?

176. **haunted:** frequented.

182. **compliments:** affectation of perfect formal courtesy.

183. **mutiny:** dispute.

184. **hight:** is named.

185. **interim:** interlude; entertainment.

187. **lost in the world's debate:** killed in various battles of the great world.

188. **How you delight:** what things delight you.

190. **minstrelsy:** amusement.

191. **wight:** person.

192. **fire-new:** freshly coined.

193. **swain:** rustic youth.

197. **reprehend:** represent. Dull, like many of Shakespeare's comic characters, gains comic effect by his misuse of words.

198. **tharborough:** thirdborough; a petty constable.

King. Ay, that there is. Our court, you know, is haunted 175
With a refined traveler of Spain,
A man in all the world's new fashion planted,
That hath a mint of phrases in his brain;
One who the music of his own vain tongue 180
Doth ravish like enchanting harmony;
A man of compliments, whom right and wrong
Have chose as umpire of their mutiny.
This child of fancy, that Armado hight,
For interim to our studies shall relate 185
In highborn words the worth of many a knight
From tawny Spain lost in the world's debate.
How you delight, my lords, I know not, I;
But I protest I love to hear him lie,
And I will use him for my minstrelsy. 190

Ber. Armado is a most illustrious wight,
A man of fire-new words, fashion's own knight.

Long. Costard the swain and he shall be our sport;
And so to study three years is but short.

Enter [Dull,] a constable, with a letter, and Costard.

Dull. Which is the Duke's own person? 195

Ber. This, fellow. What wouldst?

Dull. I myself reprehend his own person, for I am his Grace's tharborough; but I would see his own person in flesh and blood.

Ber. This is he. 200

Dull. Signior Arme—Arme—commends you. There's villainy abroad; this letter will tell you more.

203. **contempts:** contents.

205. **magnificent Armado:** probably a satirical glance at the "magnificent Armada" of Spain.

213. **style:** a pun on stile/style.

216-17. **with the manner:** in the act (of committing something forbidden). Originally the phrase meant "with stolen goods in hand."

221. **form:** bench.

233-34. **welkin:** heavens; sky; **vicegerent:** ruler by divine right.

Cost. Sir, the contempts thereof are as touching me.

King. A letter from the magnificent Armado. 205

Ber. How low soever the matter, I hope in God for high words.

Long. A high hope for a low heaven. God grant us patience!

Ber. To hear, or forbear hearing? 210

Long. To hear meekly, sir, and to laugh moderately; or to forbear both.

Ber. Well, sir, be it as the style shall give us cause to climb in the merriness.

Cost. The matter is to me, sir, as concerning 215 Jaquenetta. The manner of it is, I was taken with the manner.

Ber. In what manner?

Cost. In manner and form following, sir; all those three: I was seen with her in the manor house, sitting 220 with her upon the form, and taken following her into the park; which, put together, is in manner and form following. Now, sir, for the manner—it is the manner of a man to speak to a woman. For the form—in some form. 225

Ber. For the following, sir?

Cost. As it shall follow in my correction; and God defend the right!

King. Will you hear this letter with attention?

Ber. As we would hear an oracle. 230

Cost. Such is the simplicity of man to hearken after the flesh.

King. [*Reads*] "Great deputy, the welkin's vice-

234. **dominator:** lord.

239. **but so:** just so-so.

246-47. **commend:** commit; offer up; **black oppressing humor:** i.e., black bile, which was considered the cause of melancholy. The various body fluids were known as "humors"; **physic:** medicine.

253. **ycleped:** called.

255. **prepost'rous:** monstrous; extraordinary.

260. **curious-knotted garden:** flower beds planted in an intricate pattern.

261-62. **minnow of thy mirth:** insignificant creature whose function is to amuse you, with the implication that the amusement he can provide is slight.

A "curious-knotted garden." From Charles Estienne, *L'agriculture et maison rustique* (1583)

gerent and sole dominator of Navarre, my soul's earth's god and body's fost'ring patron"— 235

Cost. Not a word of Costard yet.

King. [*Reads*] "So it is"—

Cost. It may be so; but if he say it is so, he is, in telling true, but so.

King. Peace! 240

Cost. Be to me, and every man that dares not fight!

King. No words!

Cost. Of other men's secrets, I beseech you.

King. [*Reads*] "So it is, besieged with sable-colored 245 melancholy, I did commend the black oppressing humor to the most wholesome physic of thy health-giving air; and, as I am a gentleman, betook myself to walk. The time When? About the sixth hour; when beasts most graze, birds best peck, and men sit down 250 to that nourishment which is called supper. So much for the time When. Now for the ground Which? which, I mean, I walked upon; it is ycleped thy park. Then for the place Where? where, I mean, I did encounter that obscene and most prepost'rous event 255 that draweth from my snow-white pen the ebon-colored ink which here thou viewest, beholdest, surveyest, or seest. But to the place Where? It standeth north-north-east and by east from the west corner of thy curious-knotted garden. There did I see 260 that low-spirited swain, that base minnow of thy mirth,"

Cost. Me?

King. "that unlettered small-knowing soul,"

270. **sorted:** associated.

271. **continent canon:** restraining law.

272. **passion:** grieve.

278. **meed:** merited portion.

285. **vessel:** receptacle; that is, the object which is due to feel the fury of his law.

292. **the best for the worst:** the best example of pedantry at its worst.

Cost. Me? 265

King. "that shallow vassal,"

Cost. Still me?

King. "which, as I remember, hight Costard,"

Cost. O, me!

King. "sorted and consorted, contrary to thy estab- 270
lished proclaimed edict and continent canon; which, with, O, with—but with this I passion to say wherewith—"

Cost. With a wench.

King. "with a child of our grandmother Eve, a 275
female; or, for thy more sweet understanding, a woman. Him I, as my ever-esteemed duty pricks me on, have sent to thee, to receive the meed of punishment, by thy sweet Grace's officer, Anthony Dull, a man of good repute, carriage, bearing, and esti- 280
mation."

Dull. Me, an't shall please you; I am Anthony Dull.

King. "For Jaquenetta—so is the weaker vessel called, which I apprehended with the aforesaid swain —I keep her as a vessel of thy law's fury, and shall, 285
at the least of thy sweet notice, bring her to trial. Thine, in all compliments of devoted and heartburning heat of duty,

DON ADRIANO DE ARMADO."

Ber. This is not so well as I looked for, but the best 290
that ever I heard.

King. Ay, the best for the worst. But, sirrah, what say you to this?

Cost. Sir, I confess the wench.

313. **mutton:** in view of the foregoing enumeration of virgins, Costard probably puns on a slang meaning of **mutton:** a loose woman.

319. **lay:** wager; **goodman:** yeoman.

320. **idle scorn:** foolish mockery.

323. **true:** honest.

King. Did you hear the proclamation? 295

Cost. I do confess much of the hearing it, but little of the marking of it.

King. It was proclaimed a year's imprisonment to be taken with a wench.

Cost. I was taken with none, sir; I was taken with 300 a damsel.

King. Well, it was proclaimed damsel.

Cost. This was no damsel neither, sir; she was a virgin.

King. It is so varied too, for it was proclaimed 305 virgin.

Cost. If it were, I deny her virginity; I was taken with a maid.

King. This "maid" will not serve your turn, sir.

Cost. This maid will serve my turn, sir. 310

King. Sir, I will pronounce your sentence: you shall fast a week with bran and water.

Cost. I had rather pray a month with mutton and porridge.

King. And Don Armado shall be your keeper. 315
My Lord Berowne, see him delivered o'er;
And go we, lords, to put in practice that
Which each to other hath so strongly sworn.

[*Exeunt King, Longaville, and Dumaine*.]

Ber. I'll lay my head to any goodman's hat
These oaths and laws will prove an idle scorn. 320
Sirrah, come on.

Cost. I suffer for the truth, sir; for true it is I was taken with Jaquenetta, and Jaquenetta is a true girl;

I. [ii.] Armado confesses to his page, Moth, that he is in love with Jaquenetta. The arrival of the constable with Costard and Jaquenetta gives Armado an opportunity for a brief exchange of words with the girl, who seems indifferent to the honor of having aroused Armado's passion. The Spaniard is forced to admit to himself that he is no match for Cupid.

8. **juvenal:** youth.
9. **working:** operation.
13. **congruent:** suitable.
14. **epitheton:** epithet; term.

and therefore welcome the sour cup of prosperity!
Affliction may one day smile again; and till then, sit 325
thee down, sorrow!

Exeunt.

[Scene II. The same.]

Enter Armado and Moth, his page.

Arm. Boy, what sign is it when a man of great spirit grows melancholy?

Moth. A great sign, sir, that he will look sad.

Arm. Why, sadness is one and the selfsame thing, dear imp. 5

Moth. No, no; O Lord, sir, no!

Arm. How canst thou part sadness and melancholy, my tender juvenal?

Moth. By a familiar demonstration of the working, my tough signior. 10

Arm. Why tough signior? Why tough signior?

Moth. Why tender juvenal? Why tender juvenal?

Arm. I spoke it, tender juvenal, as a congruent epitheton appertaining to thy young days, which we may nominate tender. 15

Moth. And I, tough signior, as an appertinent title to your old time, which we may name tough.

Arm. Pretty and apt.

Moth. How mean you, sir? I pretty, and my saying apt? or I apt, and my saying pretty? 20

Arm. Thou pretty, because little.

25. **condign:** deserved.

33-4. **crosses love not him:** i.e., he never has much money. A cross was a coin, the name deriving from the cross depicted thereon.

39. **told:** counted.

43. **varnish:** outward symbol.

48. **vulgar:** common folk.

The "dancing horse," Morocco. Robert Chambers, *Book of Days* (1869). (See I. ii. 53. note)

Moth. Little pretty, because little. Wherefore apt?

Arm. And therefore apt, because quick.

Moth. Speak you this in my praise, master?

Arm. In thy condign praise. 25

Moth. I will praise an eel with the same praise.

Arm. What, that an eel is ingenious?

Moth. That an eel is quick.

Arm. I do say thou art quick in answers; thou heatst my blood. 30

Moth. I am answered, sir.

Arm. I love not to be crossed.

Moth. [*Aside*] He speaks the mere contrary: crosses love not him.

Arm. I have promised to study three years with the Duke. 35

Moth. You may do it in an hour, sir.

Arm. Impossible.

Moth. How many is one thrice told?

Arm. I am ill at reck'ning; it fitteth the spirit of a tapster. 40

Moth. You are a gentleman and a gamester, sir.

Arm. I confess both: they are both the varnish of a complete man.

Moth. Then I am sure you know how much the gross sum of deuce-ace amounts to. 45

Arm. It doth amount to one more than two.

Moth. Which the base vulgar do call three.

Arm. True.

Moth. Why, sir, is this such a piece of study? Now here is three studied ere ye'll thrice wink; and how easy it is to put "years" to the word "three," and 50

53. **the dancing horse:** a horse trained to tap out numbers with his hoof. One Banks and his horse Morocco are recorded as performing in England in the 1590's, and there may have been other horses trained in similar tricks.

55. **figure:** piece of logic.

56. **cipher:** nothing.

62-3. **new-devised curtsy:** there are many contemporary references to the importation of French manners.

66. **Hercules:** this is the first of more than half a dozen references to Hercules in the play. It is possible that Shakespeare may have known that the Kings of Navarre claimed descent from the hero Hercules.

74. **rapier:** i.e., swordplay.

78. **complexion:** Armado means **complexion** in the sense which is normally used today, but Moth at first replies in reference to her temperament. A person's complexion also meant the particular humor which governed his disposition, i.e., blood, phlegm, choler, or black choler.

Samson and Delilah. From Guillaume Rouillé, *Promptuarii iconum* (1553)

study three years in two words, the dancing horse will tell you.

Arm. A most fine figure! 55

Moth. [*Aside*] To prove you a cipher.

Arm. I will hereupon confess I am in love. And as it is base for a soldier to love, so am I in love with a base wench. If drawing my sword against the humor of affection would deliver me from the reprobate 60 thought of it, I would take Desire prisoner, and ransom him to any French courtier for a new-devised curtsy. I think scorn to sigh; methinks I should outswear Cupid. Comfort me, boy; what great men have been in love? 65

Moth. Hercules, master.

Arm. Most sweet Hercules! More authority, dear boy, name more; and, sweet my child, let them be men of good repute and carriage.

Moth. Samson, master; he was a man of good 70 carriage, great carriage, for he carried the town gates on his back like a porter; and he was in love.

Arm. O well-knit Samson! strong-jointed Samson! I do excel thee in my rapier as much as thou didst me in carrying gates. I am in love too. Who was Samson's 75 love, my dear Moth?

Moth. A woman, master.

Arm. Of what complexion?

Moth. Of all the four, or the three, or the two, or one of the four. 80

Arm. Tell me precisely of what complexion.

Moth. Of the sea-water green, sir.

Arm. Is that one of the four complexions?

88. **green:** lively.

90. **maculate:** impure.

106. **native she doth owe:** she naturally possesses.

109-10. **a ballad . . . of the King and the Beggar:** an old song about King Cophetua and the beautiful beggarmaid with whom he fell in love.

Moth. As I have read, sir; and the best of them too.

Arm. Green, indeed, is the color of lovers; but to have a love of that color, methinks Samson had small reason for it. He surely affected her for her wit. 85

Moth. It was so, sir; for she had a green wit.

Arm. My love is most immaculate white and red.

Moth. Most maculate thoughts, master, are masked under such colors. 90

Arm. Define, define, well-educated infant.

Moth. My father's wit and my mother's tongue assist me!

Arm. Sweet invocation of a child; most pretty and pathetical! 95

Moth. If she be made of white and red,
Her faults will ne'er be known;
For blushing cheeks by faults are bred, 100
And fears by pale white shown.
Then if she fear, or be to blame,
By this you shall not know;
For still her cheeks possess the same 105
Which native she doth owe.

A dangerous rhyme, master, against the reason of white and red.

Arm. Is there not a ballad, boy, of the King and the Beggar? 110

Moth. The world was very guilty of such a ballad some three ages since; but I think now 'tis not to be found; or if it were, it would neither serve for the writing nor the tune.

116. digression: deviation; straying from my normal course.

118. rational hind: i.e., stag capable of reasoning. **Hind** also meant a rustic or a clown, and both meanings are intended.

123. light: wanton.

128. suffer: permit.

129. penance: Dull probably means "pleasance," pleasure; **'a:** he.

131. allowed: permitted; **daywoman:** dairymaid.

139. With that face: Jaquenetta expresses doubt of Armado's capacity to reveal anything wonderful.

Arm. I will have that subject newly writ o'er, that I may example my digression by some mighty precedent. Boy, I do love that country girl that I took in the park with the rational hind Costard; she deserves well. 115

Moth. [*Aside*] To be whipped; and yet a better love than my master. 120

Arm. Sing, boy; my spirit grows heavy in love.

Moth. And that's great marvel, loving a light wench.

Arm. I say, sing. 125

Moth. Forbear till this company be past.

Enter Dull, Costard, and Jaquenetta.

Dull. Sir, the Duke's pleasure is that you keep Costard safe; and you must suffer him to take no delight nor no penance, but 'a must fast three days a week. For this damsel, I must keep her at the park; she is allowed for the daywoman. Fare you well. 130

Arm. I do betray myself with blushing. Maid!

Jaq. Man!

Arm. I will visit thee at the lodge.

Jaq. That's hereby. 135

Arm. I know where it is situate.

Jaq. Lord, how wise you are!

Arm. I will tell thee wonders.

Jaq. With that face?

Arm. I love thee. 140

Jaq. So I heard you say.

Arm. And so, farewell.

148. **on a full stomach:** with courage.

150. **fellows:** servants.

156. **fast and loose:** a conjurer's trick with a fake knot.

169. **argument:** proof.

171. **familiar:** evil spirit.

Jaq. Fair weather after you!

Dull. Come, Jaquenetta, away.

Exeunt [Dull and Jaquenetta].

Arm. Villain, thou shalt fast for thy offenses ere thou be pardoned. 145

Cost. Well, sir, I hope when I do it I shall do it on a full stomach.

Arm. Thou shalt be heavily punished.

Cost. I am more bound to you than your fellows, for they are but lightly rewarded. 150

Arm. Take away this villain; shut him up.

Moth. Come, you transgressing slave, away.

Cost. Let me not be pent up, sir; I will fast, being loose. 155

Moth. No, sir; that were fast and loose. Thou shalt to prison.

Cost. Well, if ever I do see the merry days of desolation that I have seen, some shall see.

Moth. What shall some see? 160

Cost. Nay, nothing, Master Moth, but what they look upon. It is not for prisoners to be too silent in their words, and therefore I will say nothing. I thank God I have as little patience as another man, and therefore I can be quiet. 165

Exeunt [Moth and Costard].

Arm. I do affect the very ground, which is base, where her shoe, which is baser, guided by her foot, which is basest, doth tread. I shall be forsworn, which is a great argument of falsehood, if I love. And how can that be true love which is falsely attempted? 170
Love is a familiar; Love is a devil; there is no evil

174. **wit:** wisdom.

174-75. **butt shaft:** practice arrow with blunt head.

176-77. **The first and second cause will not serve my turn:** i.e., the rules of honor governing the duel will not help me with Cupid; there is no use in challenging him to a duel; **passado:** from the Italian *passata,* Spanish *pasada,* pass; a sword thrust.

178. **duello:** dueling code.

179. **boy:** i.e., as though he were a servant.

angel but Love. Yet was Samson so tempted, and he had an excellent strength; yet was Solomon so seduced, and he had a very good wit. Cupid's butt shaft is too hard for Hercules' club, and therefore 175 too much odds for a Spaniard's rapier. The first and second cause will not serve my turn; the passado he respects not, the duello he regards not; his disgrace is to be called boy, but his glory is to subdue men. Adieu, valor; rust, rapier; be still, drum; for your 180 manager is in love; yea, he loveth. Assist me, some extemporal god of rhyme, for I am sure I shall turn sonnet. Devise, wit; write, pen; for I am for whole volumes in folio.

Exit.

LOVE'S LABOR'S LOST

ACT II

II[i.] The Princess and her company approach the King's park. News of the King's retreat from the world has reached them and the Princess sends Boyet to discover whether they will be admitted to the court. Her ladies, Maria, Katharine, and Rosaline, show themselves familiar with the three Lords of the King's train, who seem to have made a vivid impression upon them at a previous meeting. The King greets them; courteously declines to have them enter his court, though he will lodge them in his park; and hears the Princess' mission, which he promises to deal with justly. Berowne and Rosaline renew their acquaintance, and the other Lords are fascinated by Maria and Katharine. Boyet tells the Princess that the King is smitten with her beauty, but she dismisses the idea as a mere jest.

1. **dearest spirits:** wittiest resources.
5. **inheritor:** possessor.
6. **owe:** own.
15. **flourish:** ornament.
17. **chapmen's:** hucksters'.

ACT II

[Scene I. The same.]

Enter the Princess of France, with three attending ladies, [(*Rosaline, Maria, and Katharine*), *Boyet*], *and* [*two other*] *Lords.*

Boy. Now, madam, summon up your dearest spirits.
Consider who the King your father sends,
To whom he sends, and what's his embassy:
Yourself, held precious in the world's esteem,
To parley with the sole inheritor 5
Of all perfections that a man may owe,
Matchless Navarre; the plea of no less weight
Than Aquitaine, a dowry for a queen.
Be now as prodigal of all dear grace
As Nature was in making graces dear, 10
When she did starve the general world beside
And prodigally gave them all to you.

Prin. Good Lord Boyet, my beauty, though but mean,
Needs not the painted flourish of your praise. 15
Beauty is bought by judgment of the eye,
Not utt'red by base sale of chapmen's tongues;
I am less proud to hear you tell my worth

21. task the tasker: set a task for one who has pointed out my task.

22. fame: rumor.

24. outwear: use up; consume.

26. to's: to us; i.e., me.

29. Bold: assured.

30. best-moving fair: most persuasive on behalf of justice.

34. attend: await.

46. sovereign parts: peerless endowments.

47. arts: skills.

48. would well: would do well. A verb is understood in such constructions.

A noble Frenchwoman. From Pietro Bertelli, *Diversarum nationum habitus centum* (1594)

Than you much willing to be counted wise
In spending your wit in the praise of mine. 20
But now to task the tasker: good Boyet,
You are not ignorant all-telling fame
Doth noise abroad Navarre hath made a vow,
Till painful study shall outwear three years,
No woman may approach his silent court. 25
Therefore to's seemeth it a needful course,
Before we enter his forbidden gates,
To know his pleasure; and in that behalf,
Bold of your worthiness, we single you
As our best-moving fair solicitor. 30
Tell him the daughter of the King of France,
On serious business, craving quick dispatch,
Importunes personal conference with his Grace.
Haste, signify so much, while we attend,
Like humble-visaged suitors, his high will. 35

Boy. Proud of employment, willingly I go.

Prin. All pride is willing pride, and yours is so.

Exit Boyet.

Who are the votaries, my lòving lords,
That are vow-fellows with this virtuous duke?

1st Lord. Lord Longaville is one. 40

Prin. Know you the man?

Mar. I know him, madam; at a marriage feast,
Between Lord Perigort and the beauteous heir
Of Jaques Falconbridge, solemnized
In Normandy, saw I this Longaville. 45
A man of sovereign parts he is esteemed,
Well fitted in arts, glorious in arms;
Nothing becomes him ill that he would well.

52. **still:** always.

54. **belike:** no doubt.

58. **well-accomplished:** i.e., of fine accomplishments.

61. **Most power to do most harm, least knowing ill:** that is, his great abilities would enable him to do the greatest evil, but of all people he is most innocent of wicked knowledge.

63. **grace:** favor.

66. **to:** compared to.

69. **Berowne they call him, but a merrier man:** Rosaline is punning on the name Berowne by identifying it with "brown" (gloomy, serious).

75. **conceit's expositor:** imagination's spokesman.

The only soil of his fair virtue's gloss,
If virtue's gloss will stain with any soil, 50
Is a sharp wit matched with too blunt a will,
Whose edge hath power to cut, whose will still wills
It should none spare that come within his power.

Prin. Some merry mocking lord, belike; is't so?

Mar. They say so most that most his humors know. 55

Prin. Such short-lived wits do wither as they grow.
Who are the rest?

Kath. The young Dumaine, a well-accomplished youth,
Of all that virtue love for virtue loved; 60
Most power to do most harm, least knowing ill,
For he hath wit to make an ill shape good,
And shape to win grace though he had no wit.
I saw him at the Duke Alençon's once,
And much too little of that good I saw 65
Is my report to his great worthiness.

Ros. Another of these students at that time
Was there with him, if I have heard a truth.
Berowne they call him, but a merrier man,
Within the limit of becoming mirth, 70
I never spent an hour's talk withal.
His eye begets occasion for his wit,
For every object that the one doth catch
The other turns to a mirth-moving jest,
Which his fair tongue, conceit's expositor, 75
Delivers in such apt and gracious words
That aged ears play truant at his tales,
And younger hearings are quite ravished,
So sweet and voluble is his discourse.

81. **garnished:** adorned.
86. **competitors:** colleagues.
87. **addressed:** prepared.
92. **unpeopled:** unattended by servants.

Prin. God bless my ladies! are they all in love, 80
That every one her own hath garnished
With such bedecking ornaments of praise?
1st Lord. Here comes Boyet.

[*Re-*]*enter Boyet.*

Prin. Now, what admittance, lord?
Boy. Navarre had notice of your fair approach, 85
And he and his competitors in oath
Were all addressed to meet you, gentle lady,
Before I came. Marry, thus much I have learnt:
He rather means to lodge you in the field,
Like one that comes here to besiege his court, 90
Than seek a dispensation for his oath,
To let you enter his unpeopled house.

Enter King, Longaville, Dumaine, Berowne,
[*and Attendants*].

Here comes Navarre.
King. Fair Princess, welcome to the court of
Navarre. 95
Prin. "Fair" I give you back again; and "welcome"
I have not yet. The roof of this court is too high to be
yours, and welcome to the wide fields too base to be
mine.
King. You shall be welcome, madam, to my court. 100
Prin. I will be welcome then; conduct me thither.
King. Hear me, dear lady: I have sworn an oath—
Prin. Our Lady help my lord! He'll be forsworn.

104. **by my will:** if I can help it.

110. **sworn out:** forsworn; **housekeeping:** hospitality.

114. **beseemeth:** becomes.

116. **suddenly:** without delay.

118. **that I were away:** i.e., the sooner to bring about my departure.

121. **Ros.:** the speech prefix for the lady in this exchange with Berowne is Katharine in the Quarto and Rosaline in the Folio. The confusion may be due to alteration in the copy which the printer failed to understand. Many editors prefer Katharine because Berowne talks briefly with Rosaline again at l. 190; they conjecture that the ladies are masked and Berowne mistakes Katharine for his Rosaline. It seems incredible, however, that the ladies should wear masks here, since it is this meeting which arouses ardent passion in the four men.

125. **'long of:** along of; on account of. A colloquialism still used in some areas; **spur:** a quibble. The provincial word "speer" meant to ask questions.

King. Not for the world, fair madam, by my will.

Prin. Why, will shall break it; will, and nothing else. 105

King. Your ladyship is ignorant what it is.

Prin. Were my lord so, his ignorance were wise,
Where now his knowledge must prove ignorance.
I hear your Grace hath sworn out housekeeping. 110
'Tis deadly sin to keep that oath, my lord,
And sin to break it.
But pardon me, I am too sudden-bold;
To teach a teacher ill beseemeth me.
Vouchsafe to read the purpose of my coming, 115
And suddenly resolve me in my suit.

[*Giving a paper.*]

King. Madam, I will, if suddenly I may.

Prin. You will the sooner that I were away,
For you'll prove perjured if you make me stay.

Ber. Did not I dance with you in Brabant once? 120

Ros. Did not I dance with you in Brabant once?

Ber. I know you did.

Ros. How needless was it then to ask the question!

Ber. You must not be so quick.

Ros. 'Tis 'long of you, that spur me with such questions. 125

Ber. Your wit's too hot, it speeds too fast, 'twill tire.

Ros. Not till it leave the rider in the mire.

Ber. What time o' day?

Ros. The hour that fools should ask. 130

Ber. Now fair befall your mask!

Ros. Fair fall the face it covers!

Ber. And send you many lovers!

136. **intimate:** make known.

146. **unsatisfied:** unpaid.

154. **depart withal:** give up.

156. **gelded:** mutilated. The King refers to the fact that only part of Aquitaine is in his bond, and that part not worth one hundred thousand crowns.

163. **unseeming to:** i.e., seeming not to.

From Jean de Serres, *A General Inventory of the History of France* (1611)

Ros. Amen, so you be none.
Ber. Nay, then will I be gone. 135
King. Madam, your father here doth intimate
The payment of a hundred thousand crowns,
Being but the one half of an entire sum
Disbursed by my father in his wars.
But say that he or we, as neither have, 140
Received that sum, yet there remains unpaid
A hundred thousand more, in surety of the which,
One part of Aquitaine is bound to us,
Although not valued to the money's worth.
If, then, the King your father will restore 145
But that one half which is unsatisfied,
We will give up our right in Aquitaine,
And hold fair friendship with his Majesty.
But that, it seems, he little purposeth,
For here he doth demand to have repaid 150
A hundred thousand crowns, and not demands,
On payment of a hundred thousand crowns,
To have his title live in Aquitaine;
Which we much rather had depart withal,
And have the money by our father lent, 155
Than Aquitaine so gelded as it is.
Dear Princess, were not his requests so far
From reason's yielding, your fair self should make
A yielding 'gainst some reason in my breast,
And go well satisfied to France again. 160
Prin. You do the King my father too much wrong,
And wrong the reputation of your name,
In so unseeming to confess receipt
Of that which hath so faithfully been paid.

168. **arrest:** take for a guarantee.
169. **acquittances:** proofs of payment; receipts.
174. **specialties:** particulars; **bound:** confined.
180. **Make tender of:** offer.
187. **consort:** accompany.

King. I do protest I never heard of it; 165
And, if you prove it, I'll repay it back
Or yield up Aquitaine.

Prin. We arrest your word.
Boyet, you can produce acquittances
For such a sum from special officers 170
Of Charles, his father.

King. Satisfy me so.

Boy. So please your Grace, the packet is not come,
Where that and other specialties are bound;
Tomorrow you shall have a sight of them. 175

King. It shall suffice me; at which interview
All liberal reason I will yield unto.
Meantime, receive such welcome at my hand
As honor, without breach of honor, may
Make tender of to thy true worthiness. 180
You may not come, fair Princess, within my gates;
But here without you shall be so received
As you shall deem yourself lodged in my heart,
Though so denied fair harbor in my house.
Your own good thoughts excuse me, and farewell. 185
Tomorrow shall we visit you again.

Prin. Sweet health and fair desires consort your Grace!

King. Thy own wish wish I thee in every place.
Exit [with attendants].

Ber. Lady, I will commend you to mine own heart. 190

Ros. Pray you, do my commendations; I would be glad to see it.

Ber. I would you heard it groan.

Ros. Is the fool sick?

196. let it blood: bleed it. It is an old form of the genitive.

200. No point: not in the least, with a pun.

203. stay thanksgiving: i.e., remain long enough to thank you.

212. light in the light: unchaste if examined too closely.

Ber. Sick at the heart. 195

Ros. Alack, let it blood.

Ber. Would that do it good?

Ros. My physic says "ay."

Ber. Will you prick't with your eye?

Ros. No point, with my knife. 200

Ber. Now, God save thy life!

Ros. And yours from long living!

Ber. I cannot stay thanksgiving. [*Retiring.*]

Dum. Sir, I pray you, a word: what lady is that same? 205

Boy. The heir of Alençon, Katharine her name.

Dum. A gallant lady! Monsieur, fare you well.

Exit.

Long. I beseech you a word: what is she in the white?

Boy. A woman sometimes, an you saw her in the light. 210

Long. Perchance light in the light. I desire her name.

Boy. She hath but one for herself; to desire that were a shame. 215

Long. Pray you, sir, whose daughter?

Boy. Her mother's, I have heard.

Long. God's blessing on your beard!

Boy. Good sir, be not offended;

She is an heir of Falconbridge. 220

Long. Nay, my choler is ended.

She is a most sweet lady.

Boy. Not unlike, sir; that may be. *Exit Longaville.*

227. **or so:** or something of that sort.

233-34. **take him at his word:** jest in his own fashion and have the last word; outdo him in jesting.

243. **My lips are no common, though several they be: common** is land which is not individually owned and is farmed communally; **several** is private land, usually enclosed.

249. **bookmen:** scholars.

Ber. What's her name in the cap?
Boy. Rosaline, by good hap. 225
Ber. Is she wedded or no?
Boy. To her will, sir, or so.
Ber. You are welcome, sir; adieu!
Boy. Farewell to me, sir, and welcome to you.
Exit Berowne.
Mar. That last is Berowne, the merry madcap lord: 230
Not a word with him but a jest.
Boy. And every jest but a word.
Prin. It was well done of you to take him at his word.
Boy. I was as willing to grapple as he was to board. 235
Kath. Two hot sheeps, marry!
Boy. And wherefore not ships?
No sheep, sweet lamb, unless we feed on your lips.
Kath. You sheep and I pasture—shall that finish the jest? 240
Boy. So you grant pasture for me.
[*Offering to kiss her.*]
Kath. Not so, gentle beast.
My lips are no common, though several they be.
Boy. Belonging to whom?
Kath. To my fortunes and me. 245
Prin. Good wits will be jangling; but, gentles, agree:
This civil war of wits were much better used
On Navarre and his bookmen, for here 'tis abused.
Boy. If my observation, which very seldom lies, 250
By the heart's still rhetoric disclosed with eyes,
Deceive me not now, Navarre is infected.

256-57. **all his behaviors did make their retire/To the court of his eye:** his manners were forced to yield to the powerful effect of the sight of you; **thorough:** through.

258. **agate:** agate stone. Engraved agates were popular stones for rings.

268. **point:** direct.

269. **margent:** margin. Explanatory notes and confirming quotations from other sources were usually printed in the margins of books.

273. **disposed:** in a gay mood.

Prin. With what?

Boy. With that which we lovers entitle "affected."

Prin. Your reason? 255

Boy. Why, all his behaviors did make their retire
To the court of his eye, peeping thorough desire.
His heart, like an agate, with your print impressed,
Proud with his form, in his eye pride expressed;
His tongue, all impatient to speak and not see, 260
Did stumble with haste in his eyesight to be;
All senses to that sense did make their repair,
To feel only looking on fairest of fair.
Methought all his senses were locked in his eye,
As jewels in crystal for some prince to buy, 265
Who, tend'ring their own worth from where they
were glassed,
Did point you to buy them, along as you passed.
His face's own margent did quote such amazes
That all eyes saw his eyes enchanted with gazes. 270
I'll give you Aquitaine and all that is his,
An you give him for my sake but one loving kiss.

Prin. Come, to our pavilion: Boyet is disposed.

Boy. But to speak that in words which his eye hath
disclosed; 275
I only have made a mouth of his eye,
By adding a tongue which I know will not lie.

Mar. Thou art an old lovemonger, and speakest
skillfully.

Kath. He is Cupid's grandfather and learns news of 280
him.

Ros. Then was Venus like her mother, for her father
is but grim.

Boy. Do you hear, my mad wenches?
Mar. No. 285
Boy. What, then; do you see?
Mar. Ay, our way to be gone.
Boy. You are too hard for me.
Exeunt.

LOVE'S LABOR'S LOST

ACT III

III.[i.] The ardent Armado releases Costard so that he may bear a love letter to Jaquenetta. Before Costard can fulfill this commission, however, Berowne meets the rustic and gives him his own message for Rosaline.

3. **Concolinel:** this may suggest a trill or it may be the title of a song now forgotten sung by Moth at this point.

5-6. **festinately:** speedily.

8. **French brawl:** a dance, *bransle* in French, corrupted to **brawl.** The phrase probably also refers to the civil wars in France, which had been the chief item in news from France for some time.

11. **canary:** i.e., dance the canaries, a lively dance.

16. **penthouse-like:** i.e., tilted, like a penthouse roof.

17-18. **arms crossed:** an attitude expressing melancholy to the Elizabethans; **thin-belly doublet:** most doublets were stuffed and shaped in an exaggerated curve over the abdomen. **Thin-belly doublet** describes the wasted appearance of the languishing lover. Cf. *Henry V*, IV. vii. 47, where Fluellen describes Falstaff as "the fat knight with the great belly doublet."

20. **snip:** scrap.

ACT III

[Scene I. The same.]

Enter Armado and Moth.

Arm. Warble, child; make passionate my sense of hearing.

Moth. Concolinel.

Arm. Sweet air! Go, tenderness of years, take this key, give enlargement to the swain, bring him festinately hither; I must employ him in a letter to my love. 5

Moth. Master, will you win your love with a French brawl?

Arm. How meanest thou? Brawling in French?

Moth. No, my complete master; but to jig off a tune at the tongue's end, canary to it with your feet, humor it with turning up your eyelids, sigh a note and sing a note, sometime through the throat, as if you swallowed love with singing love, sometime through the nose, as if you snuffed up love by smelling love, with your hat penthouse-like o'er the shop of your eyes, with your arms crossed on your thin-belly doublet like a rabbit on a spit, or your hands in your pocket like a man after the old painting; and keep not too long in one tune, but a snip and away. These 10 15 20

24. affected: given; inclined.

28. the hobbyhorse is forgot: a proverbial expression, perhaps a fragment of an old song.

29. hobbyhorse: loose woman.

31. hackney: strumpet; something, like a nag, available for hire by anyone.

50. well sympathized: appropriately disposed of.

are compliments, these are humors; these betray nice wenches, that would be betrayed without these; and make them men of note (do you note, men?) that most are affected to these.

Arm. How hast thou purchased this experience? 25

Moth. By my penny of observation.

Arm. But O—but O—

Moth. "The hobbyhorse is forgot."

Arm. Callst thou my love "hobbyhorse"?

Moth. No, master; the hobbyhorse is but a colt and 30 your love perhaps a hackney. But have you forgot your love?

Arm. Almost I had.

Moth. Negligent student! learn her by heart.

Arm. By heart and in heart, boy. 35

Moth. And out of heart, master; all those three I will prove.

Arm. What wilt thou prove?

Moth. A man, if I live; and this, by, in, and without, upon the instant. By heart you love her, because your 40 heart cannot come by her; in heart you love her, because your heart is in love with her; and out of heart you love her, being out of heart that you cannot enjoy her.

Arm. I am all these three. 45

Moth. And three times as much more, and yet nothing at all.

Arm. Fetch hither the swain; he must carry me a letter.

Moth. A message well sympathized—a horse to be 50 ambassador for an ass.

52. **what sayest thou:** Armado laughs automatically, until the full import of Moth's pun strikes him.

59. **Minime:** by no means.

66. **Thump:** an imitation of the noise of the cannon's discharge.

70. **gives thee place:** gives way before thee.

72. **costard:** a slang word for head, derived from the costard apple.

74. **l'envoy:** a good-by to the reader at the end of a prose work or the concluding stanza of a poem.

76. **salve:** Costard's use of the word puns on *salve,* a Latin word for salutation, to contrast with **l'envoy.**

77. **mail:** wallet; **plantain:** a leaf used to soothe bruises.

Arm. Ha, ha!—what sayest thou?

Moth. Marry, sir, you must send the ass upon the horse, for he is very slow-gaited. But I go.

Arm. The way is but short; away. 55

Moth. As swift as lead, sir.

Arm. The meaning, pretty ingenious?
Is not lead a metal heavy, dull, and slow?

Moth. *Minime*, honest master; or rather, master, no.

Arm. I say lead is slow. 60

Moth. You are too swift, sir, to say so:
Is that lead slow which is fired from a gun?

Arm. Sweet smoke of rhetoric!
He reputes me a cannon; and the bullet, that's he;
I shoot thee at the swain. 65

Moth. Thump, then, and I flee. [*Exit.*]

Arm. A most acute juvenal; voluble and free of grace!
By thy favor, sweet welkin, I must sigh in thy face;
Most rude melancholy, valor gives thee place. 70
My herald is returned.

[*Re-*]*enter Moth with Costard.*

Moth. A wonder, master! Here's a costard broken in a shin.

Arm. Some enigma, some riddle; come, thy l'envoy; begin. 75

Cost. No egma, no riddle, no l'envoy; no salve in the mail, sir. O, sir, plantain, a plain plantain; no l'envoy, no l'envoy; no salve, sir, but a plantain!

80. **spleen:** the organ which was believed to govern laughter.

82. **inconsiderate:** thoughtless person.

88. **tofore been sain:** been heretofore said.

90-1. **The fox . . . three:** this obscure jingle may be a topical allusion. Some scholars have seen a reference to the Martin Marprelate controversy, which was a pamphlet war between the Puritans and their enemies.

Arm. By virtue, thou enforcest laughter; thy silly thought, my spleen; the heaving of my lungs provokes 80
me to ridiculous smiling. O, pardon me, my stars!
Doth the inconsiderate take salve for l'envoy, and the word "l'envoy" for a salve?

Moth. Do the wise think them other? Is not l'envoy a salve? 85

Arm. No, page, it is an epilogue or discourse to make plain
Some obscure precedence that hath tofore been sain.
I will example it:

The fox, the ape, and the humblebee, 90
Were still at odds, being but three.

There's the moral: now the l'envoy.

Moth. I will add the l'envoy. Say the moral again.

Arm. The fox, the ape, and the humblebee,
Were still at odds, being but three. 95

Moth. Until the goose came out of door,
And stayed the odds by adding four.
Now will I begin your moral, and do you follow with my l'envoy.

The fox, the ape, and the humblebee, 100
Were still at odds, being but three.

Arm. Until the goose came out of door,
Staying the odds by adding four.

Moth. A good l'envoy, ending in the goose; would you desire more? 105

Cost. The boy hath sold him a bargain, a goose, that's flat.
Sir, your pennyworth is good, an your goose be fat.

119. **And he ended the market:** a reference to a popular proverb: Three women and a goose make a market.

129. **enfranchise:** free.

131. **goose:** prostitute.

139. **significant:** token (a letter).

To sell a bargain well is as cunning as fast and loose;
Let me see: a fat l'envoy; ay, that's a fat goose. 110

Arm. Come hither, come hither. How did this argument begin?

Moth. By saying that a costard was broken in a shin.
Then called you for the l'envoy. 115

Cost. True, and I for a plantain. Thus came your argument in;
Then the boy's fat l'envoy, the goose that you bought;
And he ended the market.

Arm. But tell me: how was there a costard broken 120 in a shin?

Moth. I will tell you sensibly.

Cost. Thou hast no feeling of it, Moth; I will speak that l'envoy.
I, Costard, running out, that was safely within, 125
Fell over the threshold and broke my shin.

Arm. We will talk no more of this matter.

Cost. Till there be more matter in the shin.

Arm. Sirrah Costard, I will enfranchise thee.

Cost. O, marry me to one Frances! I smell some 130 l'envoy, some goose, in this.

Arm. By my sweet soul, I mean setting thee at liberty, enfreedoming thy person; thou wert immured, restrained, captivated, bound.

Cost. True, true; and now you will be my purga- 135 tion, and let me loose.

Arm. I give thee thy liberty, set thee from durance; and, in lieu thereof, impose on thee nothing but this: bear this significant [*Giving a letter*] to the country

141. **ward:** defense; guard.

144. **incony:** rare; remarkable. The derivation of this slang word is unknown.

145. **Jew:** a complimentary epithet of uncertain meaning.

148. **inkle:** a kind of tape.

A night-watch constable. From Thomas Dekker, *The Bellman of London* (1608) (See III. i. 186)

maid Jaquenetta; there is remuneration, for the best 140
ward of mine honor is rewarding my dependents.
Moth, follow. [*Exit.*]

Moth. Like the sequel, I. Signior Costard, adieu.
Exit [*Moth*].

Cost. My sweet ounce of man's flesh, my incony
Jew! Now will I look to his remuneration. Remunera- 145
tion! O, that's the Latin word for three farthings.
Three farthings—remuneration. "What's the price of
this inkle?"—"One penny."—"No, I'll give you a remuneration." Why, it carries it. Remuneration! Why,
it is a fairer name than French crown. I will never 150
buy and sell out of this word.

Enter Berowne.

Ber. My good knave Costard, exceedingly well met!

Cost. Pray you, sir, how much carnation ribbon
may a man buy for a remuneration?

Ber. What is a remuneration? 155

Cost. Marry, sir, halfpenny farthing.

Ber. Why, then, three-farthing worth of silk.

Cost. I thank your worship. God be wi' you!

Ber. Stay, slave, I must employ thee.
As thou wilt win my favor, good my knave, 160
Do one thing for me that I shall entreat.

Cost. When would you have it done, sir?

Ber. This afternoon.

Cost. Well, I will do it, sir; fare you well.

Ber. Thou knowest not what it is. 165

Cost. I shall know, sir, when I have done it.

178. **guerdon:** reward.

180. **a 'leven-pence farthing:** eleven and a quarter pennies. Berowne has given Costard a shilling, which is worth twelve pence.

181. **in print:** to the letter.

185. **beadle:** an official who saw to the punishment of rogues, strumpets, and other offenders; **humorous:** melancholy.

188. **magnificent:** vainglorious.

189. **wimpled:** referring to pictures of Cupid with a cloth over his eyes to indicate love's blindness; **purblind:** totally blind.

190. **Signior junior: Signior** as a title to show Cupid's distinction; **junior** indicating that he is a little boy; **Dan:** a corruption of the Latin word *dominus*, master or sir.

191. **folded arms:** see note above, ll. 17-18.

194. **plackets:** petticoats, hence, women.

196. **paritors:** officers who served summonses on behalf of the ecclesiastical authority, often for sexual offenses.

Ber. Why, villain, thou must know first.

Cost. I will come to your worship tomorrow morning.

Ber. It must be done this afternoon. 17
Hark, slave, it is but this:
The Princess comes to hunt here in the park,
And in her train there is a gentle lady;
When tongues speak sweetly, then they name her name, 17
And Rosaline they call her. Ask for her,
And to her white hand see thou do commend
This sealed-up counsel. There's thy guerdon; go.

Cost. Gardon, O sweet gardon! better than remuneration; a 'leven-pence farthing better; most sweet 18
gardon! I will do it, sir, in print. Gardon—remuneration! *Exit.*

Ber. And I, forsooth, in love! I, that have been love's whip!
A very beadle to a humorous sigh; 18
A critic, nay, a night-watch constable;
A domineering pedant o'er the boy,
Than whom no mortal so magnificent!
This wimpled, whining, purblind, wayward boy,
This Signior junior, giant-dwarf, Dan Cupid; 19
Regent of love rhymes, lord of folded arms,
The anointed sovereign of sighs and groans,
Liege of all loiterers and malcontents,
Dread prince of plackets, king of codpieces,
Sole imperator, and great general 19
Of trotting paritors. O my little heart!
And I to be a corporal of his field,

198. **wear his colors like a tumbler's hoop:** i.e., flaunt tokens of my allegiance to him.

202-3. **never going aright . . . /But being watched that it may still go right:** never acting properly unless constantly watched to see that it does.

206. **whitely:** pale.

209. **Argus:** the monster with a hundred eyes, sent by Juno to guard Io from Jove's attentions.

210. **watch:** stay awake; spend sleepless nights.

211. **Go to:** come, come; an exclamation of resigned vexation.

215. **Some men must love my lady, and some Joan:** proverbial: Joan [any woman] is as good as my lady in the dark.

Argus lulled to sleep by Mercury. From Gabriel Simeoni, *La vita et Metamorfoseo d'Ovidio* (1559)

And wear his colors like a tumbler's hoop!
What! I love, I sue, I seek a wife—
A woman, that is like a German clock, 200
Still a-repairing, ever out of frame,
And never going aright, being a watch,
But being watched that it may still go right!
Nay, to be perjured, which is worst of all;
And, among three, to love the worst of all, 205
A whitely wanton with a velvet brow,
With two pitch balls stuck in her face for eyes;
Ay, and, by heaven, one that will do the deed,
Though Argus were her eunuch and her guard.
And I to sigh for her! to watch for her! 210
To pray for her! Go to; it is a plague
That Cupid will impose for my neglect
Of his almighty dreadful little might.
Well, I will love, write, sigh, pray, sue, and groan:
Some men must love my lady, and some Joan. 215

[*Exit.*]

LOVE'S LABOR'S LOST

ACT IV

IV.[i.] The ladies are preparing for a deer hunt when Costard appears and delivers to the Princess the letter intended for Jaquenetta. He tells them, however, that it was sent by Berowne to Rosaline, which gives Boyet a pretext to tease Rosaline about her suitor.

---

19. **never paint me:** don't gloss over my beauty.

ACT IV

[Scene I. The same.]

Enter the Princess, her ladies [(Rosaline, Maria, Katharine,) Boyet], Lords, and a Forester.

Prin. Was that the King that spurred his horse so hard
Against the steep-up rising of the hill?
Boy. I know not; but I think it was not he.
Prin. Whoe'er 'a was, 'a showed a mounting mind. 5
Well, lords, today we shall have our dispatch;
On Saturday we will return to France.
Then, forester, my friend, where is the bush
That we must stand and play the murderer in?
For. Hereby, upon the edge of yonder coppice; 10
A stand where you may make the fairest shoot.
Prin. I thank my beauty I am fair that shoot,
And thereupon thou speakst the fairest shoot.
For. Pardon me, madam, for I meant not so.
Prin. What, what? first praise me, and again say no? 15
O short-lived pride! Not fair? Alack for woe!
For. Yes, madam, fair.
Prin. Nay, never paint me now;

21. **good my glass:** my faithful mirror (addressed to the Forester).

24. **by merit:** for the sake of a reward. There is also a reference to the doctrine of salvation through good works and the contrasting belief of the Protestants that salvation came only from grace.

25. **heresy . . . fit for these days:** possibly an allusion to Henry of Navarre's conversion to Catholicism on July 25, 1593.

26. **foul:** ugly.

33. **out of question:** doubtless.

39. **curst:** shrewish.

45. **God dig-you-den:** God give you a good even.

Where fair is not, praise cannot mend the brow.
Here, good my glass, take this for telling true:
[*Giving him money.*]
Fair payment for foul words is more than due.

For. Nothing but fair is that which you inherit.

Prin. See, see, my beauty will be saved by merit.
O heresy in fair, fit for these days!
A giving hand, though foul, shall have fair praise.
But come, the bow. Now mercy goes to kill,
And shooting well is then accounted ill;
Thus will I save my credit in the shoot:
Not wounding, pity would not let me do't;
If wounding, then it was to show my skill,
That more for praise than purpose meant to kill.
And, out of question, so it is sometimes:
Glory grows guilty of detested crimes,
When, for fame's sake, for praise, an outward part,
We bend to that the working of the heart;
As I for praise alone now seek to spill
The poor deer's blood that my heart means no ill.

Boy. Do not curst wives hold that self-sovereignty
Only for praise sake, when they strive to be
Lords o'er their lords?

Prin. Only for praise; and praise we may afford
To any lady that subdues a lord.

Enter Costard.

Boy. Here comes a member of the commonwealth.

Cost. God dig-you-den all! Pray you, which is the head lady?

64. capon: love letter, probably by analogy with the French *poulet*, which means both "chicken" and "billet-doux."

74. magnanimous: noble-spirited.

75. illustrate: illustrious.

76. indubitate: undoubted.

77. Veni, vidi, vici: the words of Julius Cæsar announcing a victory.

Prin. Thou shalt know her, fellow, by the rest that have no heads.

Cost. Which is the greatest lady, the highest?

Prin. The thickest and the tallest. 5

Cost. The thickest and the tallest! It is so; truth is truth.

An your waist, mistress, were as slender as my wit,

One o' these maids' girdles for your waist should be fit. 5

Are not you the chief woman? You are the thickest here.

Prin. What's your will, sir? What's your will?

Cost. I have a letter from Monsieur Berowne to one Lady Rosaline. 6

Prin. O, thy letter, thy letter! He's a good friend of mine.

Stand aside, good bearer. Boyet, you can carve.

Break up this capon.

Boy. I am bound to serve. 6

This letter is mistook; it importeth none here.

It is writ to Jaquenetta.

Prin. We will read it, I swear.

Break the neck of the wax, and every one give ear.

Boy. [*Reads*] "By heaven, that thou art fair is most 7 infallible; true that thou art beauteous; truth itself that thou art lovely. More fairer than fair, beautiful than beauteous, truer than truth itself, have commiseration on thy heroical vassal. The magnanimous and most illustrate King Cophetua set eye upon the 7 pernicious and indubitate beggar Zenelophon; and he it was that might rightly say, *Veni, vidi, vici;* which

78. **annothanize:** a jargon term coined by Armado, by which he evidently means "annotate"; **vulgar:** vulgar tongue; English.

79. **videlicet:** that is to say.

86. **catastrophe:** final result.

92. **tittles:** dots or small marks in printing; or in other words, trifles.

96. **industry:** gallantry.

98. **the Nemean lion:** the supposedly invulnerable lion slain by Hercules as one of his labors.

108. **I am much deceived but:** unless I am much deceived.

Hercules. From *The Famous and Renowned History of the Life and Glorious Actions of the Mighty Hercules of Greece* (1719)

to annothanize in the vulgar—O base and obscure vulgar!—videlicet, He came, saw, and overcame. He came, one; saw, two; overcame, three. Who came?— 8
the king. Why did he come?—to see. Why did he see? —to overcome. To whom came he?—to the beggar. What saw he?—the beggar. Who overcame he?—the beggar. The conclusion is victory. On whose side?—
the king's. The captive is enriched. On whose side? 8
—the beggar's. The catastrophe is a nuptial. On whose side?—the king's. No, on both in one, or one in both. I am the king, for so stands the comparison; thou the beggar, for so witnesseth thy lowliness. Shall
I command thy love? I may. Shall I enforce thy love? 9
I could. Shall I entreat thy love? I will. What shalt thou exchange for rags?—robes; for tittles?—titles; for thyself?—me. Thus expecting thy reply, I profane my lips on thy foot, my eyes on thy picture, and my heart
on thy every part. 9

Thine in the dearest design of industry,

DON ADRIANO DE ARMADO.

Thus dost thou hear the Nemean lion roar
'Gainst thee, thou lamb, that standest as his prey;
Submissive fall his princely feet before, 10
And he from forage will incline to play.
But if thou strive, poor soul, what are thou then?
Food for his rage, repasture for his den."

Prin. What plume of feathers is he that indited
this letter? 10
What vane? What weathercock? Did you ever hear
better?

Boy. I am much deceived but I remember the style.

109-10. **going o'er it erewhile:** another pun on style/stile; see I. [i.] 213.

113. **phantasime:** probably, a fantastic; a person charactcrized by extravagant affectations; **Monarcho:** a well-known fantastic who frequented the court of Elizabeth.

128. **suitor:** often pronounced "shooter" and so spelled in the Quarto and Folio. This enables Rosaline to pretend to misunderstand Boyet.

130. **continent:** container.

135. **horns that year miscarry:** a favorite Elizabethan joke. **Horns** were said to be the sign of a cuckold (husband whose wife was unfaithful). Boyet means that Rosaline will quickly betray her own husband.

137-38. **shooter . . . deer:** a pun on "suitor" and "dear."

Prin. Else your memory is bad, going o'er it erewhile. 110

Boy. This Armado is a Spaniard, that keeps here in court;
A phantasime, a Monarcho, and one that makes sport
To the Prince and his bookmates.

Prin. Thou fellow, a word. 115
Who gave thee this letter?

Cost. I told you: my lord.

Prin. To whom shouldst thou give it?

Cost. From my lord to my lady.

Prin. From which lord to which lady? 120

Cost. From my Lord Berowne, a good master of mine,
To a lady of France that he called Rosaline.

Prin. Thou hast mistaken his letter. Come, lords, away. 125
[*To Rosaline*] Here, sweet, put up this; 'twill be thine another day.

Exeunt [*Princess and Train*].

Boy. Who is the suitor? who is the suitor?

Ros. Shall I teach you to know?

Boy. Ay, my continent of beauty. 130

Ros. Why, she that bears the bow.
Finely put off!

Boy. My lady goes to kill horns; but, if thou marry,
Hang me by the neck if horns that year miscarry. 135
Finely put on!

Ros. Well then, I am the shooter.

Boy. And who is your deer?

142. **still:** always.

143. **strikes at the brow:** has unerring aim; is deadly in repartee.

146. **come upon:** assault.

147. **King Pepin:** the first Carolingian king.

148. **the hit it:** a song that was sung while dancing.

150. **Queen Guinever:** wife of King Arthur. A reference to indefinite antiquity.

162. **prick:** spot in the center, equivalent to a bull's-eye; **mete:** aim.

163. **Wide o' the bow hand:** a wild shot.

166. **clout:** the peg in the center of the target that fastened it to an upright; hence, the central point.

King Pepin. From Jean de Serres, *A General Inventory of the History of France* (1611)

Ros. If we choose by the horns, yourself come not near. 140
Finely put on indeed!

Mar. You still wrangle with her, Boyet, and she strikes at the brow.

Boy. But she herself is hit lower. Have I hit her now? 145

Ros. Shall I come upon thee with an old saying, that was a man when King Pepin of France was a little boy, as touching the hit it?

Boy. So I may answer thee with one as old, that was a woman when Queen Guinever of Britain was 150 a little wench, as touching the hit it.

Ros. [*Singing*]
Thou canst not hit it, hit it, hit it,
Thou canst not hit it, my good man.

Boy. An I cannot, cannot, cannot,
An I cannot, another can. 155

[*Exeunt Rosaline and Katharine.*]

Cost. By my troth, most pleasant! How both did fit it!

Mar. A mark marvelous well shot; for they both did hit it.

Boy. A mark! O, mark but that mark! A mark, 160 says my lady!
Let the mark have a prick in't, to mete at, if it may be.

Mar. Wide o' the bow hand! I' faith, your hand is out.

Cost. Indeed, 'a must shoot nearer, or he'll ne'er 165 hit the clout.

169. **upshoot:** best shot.

170. **pin:** i.e., the clout.

175. **too much rubbing:** too many obstacles. In bowling terminology a **rub** is something that deflects the bowl from its straight course.

180. **obscenely:** Costard means some synonym for "appropriately," but the word he uses accurately describes the conversation.

182. **a the one side:** for example. Costard is contrasting Armado's behavior with women with that of Boyet, to the latter's disadvantage.

187. **pathetical:** presumably Costard means something complimentary, but he is never very clear about the precise meaning of the words he uses; **nit:** mite; tiny creature.

188. **Sola:** a hunting cry in response to an offstage shout indicating that the deer hunt is in progress.

Boy. An if my hand be out, then belike your hand is in.

Cost. Then will she get the upshoot by cleaving the pin. 170

Mar. Come, come, you talk greasily; your lips grow foul.

Cost. She's too hard for you at pricks, sir; challenge her to bowl.

Boy. I fear too much rubbing. Good night, my good owl. [*Exeunt Boyet and Maria.*] 175

Cost. By my soul, a swain, a most simple clown!
Lord, Lord! how the ladies and I have put him down!
O' my troth, most sweet jests, most incony vulgar wit!
When it comes so smoothly off, so obscenely, as it were, so fit. 180
Armado a the one side—O, most dainty man!
To see him walk before a lady and to bear her fan!
To see him kiss his hand, and how most sweetly 'a will swear! 185
And his page a tother side, that handful of wit!
Ah, heavens, it is a most pathetical nit!
Sola, sola! *A shout within.*
Exit Costard.

IV. [ii.] Holofernes, a pedantic schoolmaster, Sir Nathaniel, a country curate, and Dull, the constable, have a learned discussion of deer hunting. Jaquenetta and Costard find them and Jaquenetta asks Holofernes to read the letter (sent by Berowne to Rosaline) which Costard has given her.

---

3. **in blood:** in prime condition.

4. **pomewater:** a variety of apple.

6. **crab:** crab apple.

10. **of the first head:** five years old.

11. **Sir:** an honorary title, meaning the equivalent of the Latin *dominus*, given to all clergy as due to holders of the bachelor of arts degree; **haud credo:** I do not think so. The unlettered Dull misunderstands and protests that it was not a "doe."

12. **pricket:** buck of the second year.

19. **insert again my haud credo for a deer:** repeat his error of understanding *haud credo* to be my term for a deer.

22. **Twice-sod simplicity:** twice-repeated stupidity. **Sod** means "stewed." See the proverb "Cabbage twice cooked (sodden) is death." *Bis coctus* is the Latin for twice-cooked.

[Scene II. The same.]

Enter Holofernes, the pedant, [Sir] Nathaniel, and Dull.

Nath. Very reverent sport, truly; and done in the testimony of a good conscience.

Hol. The deer was, as you know, *sanguis,* in blood; ripe as the pomewater who now hangeth like a jewel in the ear of *caelo,* the sky, the welkin, the heaven, 5 and anon falleth like a crab on the face of *terra,* the soil, the land, the earth.

Nath. Truly, Master Holofernes, the epithets are sweetly varied, like a scholar at the least; but, sir, I assure ye it was a buck of the first head. 10

Hol. Sir Nathaniel, *haud credo.*

Dull. 'Twas not a haud credo; 'twas a pricket.

Hol. Most barbarous intimation! yet a kind of insinuation, as it were, *in via,* in way, of explication; *facere,* as it were, replication, or rather, *ostentare,* to 15 show, as it were, his inclination, after his undressed, unpolished, uneducated, unpruned, untrained, or rather unlettered, or ratherest unconfirmed fashion, to insert again my *haud credo* for a deer.

Dull. I said the deer was not a haud credo; 'twas 20 a pricket.

Hol. Twice-sod simplicity, *bis coctus!*
O thou monster Ignorance, how deformed dost thou look!

Nath. Sir, he hath never fed of the dainties that 25 are bred in a book;

36. **a patch set on learning:** a fool assigned the task of learning.

38. **omne bene:** all's well.

47. **Phoebe:** another name for Diana as moon goddess.

50. **raught:** reached.

52. **The allusion holds in the exchange:** i.e., the joke is just as good if Adam is substituted for Cain. The moon never ages beyond four weeks.

55. **capacity:** understanding.

He hath not eat paper, as it were; he hath not drunk ink; his intellect is not replenished; he is only an animal, only sensible in the duller parts;
And such barren plants are set before us that we thankful should be— 30
Which we of taste and feeling are—for those parts that do fructify in us more than he.
For as it would ill become me to be vain, indiscreet, or a fool, 35
So were there a patch set on learning to see him in a school.
But, *omne bene*, say I, being of an old father's mind:
Many can brook the weather that love not the wind.

Dull. You two are bookmen: can you tell me by your wit 40
What was a month old at Cain's birth that's not five weeks old as yet?

Hol. Dictynna, goodman Dull; Dictynna, goodman Dull. 45

Dull. What is Dictynna?

Nath. A title to Phoebe, to Luna, to the moon.

Hol. The moon was a month old when Adam was no more,
And raught not to five weeks when he came to five-score. 50
The allusion holds in the exchange.

Dull. 'Tis true, indeed; the collusion holds in the exchange.

Hol. God comfort thy capacity! I say the allusion holds in the exchange. 55

Dull. And I say the pollusion holds in the exchange;

63. **Perge:** proceed.

64. **abrogate scurrility:** omit improper language.

65. **something affect the letter:** incline somewhat to alliterative language.

69. **sore:** four-year-old deer.

71. **sorel:** a young buck.

75. **L:** the Latin numeral for fifty.

80. **talent:** a variant spelling of "talon."

81. **claws:** claw also means "flatter."

86. **pia mater:** the brain.

Mantuan. From Jean Jacques Boissard, *Icones quinquaginta virorum* (1597). (See IV. ii. 109-13)

for the moon is never but a month old; and I say, beside, that 'twas a pricket that the Princess killed.

Hol. Sir Nathaniel, will you hear an extemporal epitaph on the death of the deer? And, to humor the ignorant, call the deer the Princess killed a pricket. 60

Nath. Perge, good Master Holofernes, *perge,* so it shall please you to abrogate scurrility.

Hol. I will something affect the letter, for it argues facility. 65

The preyful Princess pierced and pricked a pretty pleasing pricket.
Some say a sore; but not a sore till now made sore with shooting. 70
The dogs did yell; put el to sore, then sorel jumps from thicket;
Or pricket sore, or else sorel; the people fall a-hooting.
If sore be sore, then L to sore makes fifty sores o' sorel. 75
Of one sore I an hundred make by adding but one more L.

Nath. A rare talent!

Dull. [*Aside*] If a talent be a claw, look how he claws him with a talent. 80

Hol. This is a gift that I have, simple, simple; a foolish extravagant spirit, full of forms, figures, shapes, objects, ideas, apprehensions, motions, revolutions. These are begot in the ventricle of memory, nourished in the womb of pia mater, and delivered upon the mellowing of occasion. But the gift is good in those in whom it is acute, and I am thankful for it. 85

93. **Mehercle:** by Hercules.

95-6. **vir sapit qui pauca loquitur:** the wise man speaks few words.

97. **Person:** a variant form of Parson.

98. **quasi:** as it were.

99. **pierced:** pronounced "persed."

102. **Piercing a hogshead:** i.e., tapping a keg of liquor. Costard has also made a pun on **hogshead,** which was used of people in the sense "blockhead"; **a good luster of conceit:** a fairly bright metaphor.

103. **turf of earth:** that is, clod.

108-9. **Fauste, precor gelida quando pecus omne sub umbra ruminat:** the beginning of the first eclogue of Battista Spagnuoli Mantuanus, known as Mantuan, a writer of pastoral poetry.

111-12. **Venetia, Venetia,/Chi non ti vede, non ti pretia:** Venice, Venice, whoso seeth thee not, values thee not.

114. **Ut, re, sol, la, mi, fa:** notes of the old scale, recited in the wrong order. "Do" was later substituted for "ut."

Nath. Sir, I praise the Lord for you, and so may my parishioners; for their sons are well tutored by 90 you, and their daughters profit very greatly under you. You are a good member of the commonwealth.

Hol. Mehercle! if their sons be ingenious, they shall want no instruction; if their daughters be capable, I will put it to them; but, *vir sapit qui pauca* 95 *loquitur.* A soul feminine saluteth us.

Enter Jaquenetta and Costard.

Jaq. God give you good morrow, Master Person.

Hol. Master Person, *quasi* pers-one. And if one should be pierced, which is the one?

Cost. Marry, Master Schoolmaster, he that is likest 100 to a hogshead.

Hol. Piercing a hogshead! A good luster of conceit in a turf of earth; fire enough for a flint, pearl enough for a swine; 'tis pretty; it is well.

Jaq. Good Master Person, be so good as read me 105 this letter; it was given me by Costard, and sent me from Don Armado. I beseech you, read it.

Hol. Fauste, precor gelida quando pecus omne sub umbra ruminat—and so forth. Ah, good old Mantuan! I may speak of thee as the traveler doth of Venice: 110

Venetia, Venetia,
Chi non ti vede, non ti pretia.

Old Mantuan! old Mantuan! Who understandeth thee not, loves thee not—Ut, re, sol, la, mi, fa. Under pardon, sir, what are the contents? or, rather, as 115 Horace says in his— What, my soul, verses?

118-19. **lege, domine:** read, sir.

124. **osiers:** willows.

126. **Study his bias leaves:** i.e., the student abandons his normal pursuit; **makes his book thine eyes:** studies only your eyes.

132. **wonder:** admiration.

133. **parts:** endowments of mind and body.

140. **apostrophus:** presumably Holofernes means that Nathaniel has pronounced "bowed" and "vowed" as two syllables.

141. **supervise:** look over; **canzonet:** verse.

142. **numbers ratified:** verses of regular meter.

143. **caret:** it is wanting.

145-46. **jerks of invention:** clever sallies; **Imitari:** to imitate.

Nath. Ay, sir, and very learned.

Hol. Let me hear a staff, a stanze, a verse; *lege, domine.*

Nath. [*Reads*] "If love make me forsworn, how shall I swear to love? 120

Ah, never faith could hold, if not to beauty vowed!
Though to myself forsworn, to thee I'll faithful prove;
Those thoughts to me were oaks, to thee like osiers bowed. 125
Study his bias leaves, and makes his book thine eyes,
Where all those pleasures live that art would comprehend.
If knowledge be the mark, to know thee shall suffice;
Well learned is that tongue that well can thee commend; 130
All ignorant that soul that sees thee without wonder;
Which is to me some praise that I thy parts admire.
Thy eye Jove's lightning bears, thy voice his dreadful thunder, 135
Which, not to anger bent, is music and sweet fire.
Celestial as thou art, O, pardon love this wrong,
That sings heaven's praise with such an earthly tongue."

Hol. You find not the apostrophus, and so miss the 140 accent. Let me supervise the canzonet. Here are only numbers ratified; but, for the elegancy, facility, and golden cadence of poesy, *caret.* Ovidius Naso was the man. And why, indeed, "Naso" but for smelling out the odoriferous flowers of fancy, the jerks of inven- 145 tion? *Imitari* is nothing: so doth the hound his master,

151. **superscript:** superscription; address.

153. **intellect:** significance; contents.

158. **sequent:** follower; attendant.

162-63. **Stay not thy compliment; I forgive thy duty:** don't delay to make your manners; I will excuse you from making a curtsy.

166. **Have with thee:** let's be off.

169-70. **colorable colors:** convincing falsehoods. **Colors** means literally "pretexts," "excuses." Holofernes places little faith in the wisdom of the "fathers" of the church.

172. **Marvelous well for the pen:** that is, he approves the handwriting but not the composition.

the ape his keeper, the tired horse his rider. But, damosella virgin, was this directed to you?

Jaq. Ay, sir, from one Monsieur Berowne, one of the strange queen's lords. 150

Hol. I will overglance the superscript: "To the snow-white hand of the most beauteous Lady Rosaline." I will look again on the intellect of the letter, for the nomination of the party writing to the person written unto: "Your Ladyship's in all desired employment, Berowne." Sir Nathaniel, this Berowne is one of the votaries with the King; and here he hath framed a letter to a sequent of the stranger queen's which accidentally, or by the way of progression, hath miscarried. Trip and go, my sweet; deliver this paper into the royal hand of the King; it may concern much. Stay not thy compliment; I forgive thy duty. Adieu. 155 160

Jaq. Good Costard, go with me. Sir, God save your life! 165

Cost. Have with thee, my girl.

Exeunt [*Costard and Jaquenetta.*]

Nath. Sir, you have done this in the fear of God, very religiously; and, as a certain father saith—

Hol. Sir, tell not me of the father; I do fear colorable colors. But to return to the verses: did they please you, Sir Nathaniel? 170

Nath. Marvelous well for the pen.

Hol. I do dine today at the father's of a certain pupil of mine; where, if, before repast, it shall please you to gratify the table with a grace, I will, on my privilege I have with the parents of the foresaid child 175

177. **ben venuto:** welcome.

185. **pauca verba:** literally, few words. "Let's say no more about it."

IV.[**iii.**] Berowne reads over some verses he has written in praise of Rosaline. One by one the King, Longaville, and Dumaine come along and reveal their own passions, unaware that they are being overheard. Berowne's guilt is also discovered when Jaquenetta and Costard return the letter to Rosaline. The four lovers resolve to forget their vows and press their suits with the ladies.

1-2. **coursing:** pursuing; chasing; **pitched a toil:** laid a trap.

6. **Ajax:** when the arms of Achilles were awarded to Ulysses instead of to himself the hero Ajax went mad and slaughtered a herd of sheep, mistaking them for his enemies.

Ajax killing himself. From Lodovico Dolce, *Le trasformationi* (1570)

or pupil, undertake your *ben venuto;* where I will prove those verses to be very unlearned, neither savoring of poetry, wit, nor invention. I beseech your society. 180

Nath. And thank you too; for society, saith the text, is the happiness of life.

Hol. And certes, the text most infallibly concludes it. [*To Dull*] Sir, I do invite you too; you shall not say me nay: *pauca verba.* Away; the gentles are at 185 their game, and we will to our recreation.

Exeunt.

[Scene III. The same.]

Enter Berowne, with a paper in his hand, alone.

Ber. The King he is hunting the deer: I am coursing myself. They have pitched a toil: I am toiling in a pitch—pitch that defiles. Defile! a foul word! Well, "set thee down, sorrow!" for so they say the fool said, and so say I, and I am the fool. Well proved, wit. By 5 the Lord, this love is as mad as Ajax: it kills sheep; it kills me—I a sheep. Well proved again o' my side! I will not love; if I do, hang me. I' faith, I will not! O, but her eye! By this light, but for her eye, I would not love her—yes, for her two eyes. Well, I do noth- 10 ing in the world but lie, and lie in my throat. By heaven, I do love; and it hath taught me to rhyme, and to be melancholy; and here is part of my rhyme, and here my melancholy. Well, she hath one o' my

22. birdbolt: a blunt missile used to kill birds.

sonnets already. The clown bore it, the fool sent it, 15
and the lady hath it: sweet clown, sweeter fool,
sweetest lady! By the world, I would not care a pin
if the other three were in. Here comes one with a
paper; God give him grace to groan!

He stands aside.

Enter the King [with a paper].

King. Ay me! 20

Ber. Shot, by heaven! Proceed, sweet Cupid; thou
hast thumped him with thy birdbolt under the left
pap. In faith, secrets!

King. [*Reads*] "So sweet a kiss the golden sun
gives not 25
To those fresh morning drops upon the rose,
As thy eyebeams, when their fresh rays have smote
The night of dew that on my cheeks down flows;
Nor shines the silver moon one half so bright
Through the transparent bosom of the deep, 30
As doth thy face through tears of mine give light.
Thou shinest in every tear that I do weep;
No drop but as a coach doth carry thee;
So ridest thou triumphing in my woe.
Do but behold the tears that swell in me, 35
And they thy glory through my grief will show.
But do not love thyself; then thou wilt keep
My tears for glasses, and still make me weep.
O queen of queens! how far dost thou excel
No thought can think nor tongue of mortal tell." 40

53. **cornercap:** biretta; the three-cornered cap of the scholar.

54. **The shape of . . . Tyburn:** i.e., triangular, like the gallows at Tyburn, a noted place of execution.

58. **numbers:** verses, as at IV.[ii.] 142.

59. **guards:** trimmings; decorations; **hose:** breeches and stockings.

60. **slop:** a term for full breeches.

How shall she know my griefs? I'll drop the paper—
Sweet leaves, shade folly. Who is he comes here?
Steps aside.

Enter Longaville [with a paper].

What, Longaville, and reading! Listen, ear.
Ber. Now, in thy likeness, one more fool appear!
Long. Ay me, I am forsworn! 45
Ber. Why, he comes in like a perjure, wearing papers.
King. In love, I hope; sweet fellowship in shame!
Ber. One drunkard loves another of the name.
Long. Am I the first that have been perjured so? 50
Ber. I could put thee in comfort: not by two that I know;
Thou makest the triumviry, the cornercap of society,
The shape of Love's Tyburn that hangs up simplicity.
Long. I fear these stubborn lines lack power to move. 55
O sweet Maria, empress of my love!
These numbers will I tear, and write in prose.
Ber. O, rhymes are guards on wanton Cupid's hose:
Disfigure not his slop. 60
Long. This same shall go.
He reads the sonnet.
"Did not the heavenly rhetoric of thine eye,
'Gainst whom the world cannot hold argument,
Persuade my heart to this false perjury?
Vows for thee broke deserve not punishment. 65

76. the liver-vein: love's very style. The liver was supposed to be the seat of passionate love.

86. woodcocks: fools.

90. she is not, corporal: there you lie: that is, Rosaline, not Katharine, is the "wonder." Dumaine is called "corporal" as being the champion of a lady.

91. Her amber hair for foul hath amber quoted: i.e., her hair puts to shame the color of amber.

92. was well noted: would be well worth noting.

A woman I forswore, but I will prove,
  Thou being a goddess, I forswore not thee:
My vow was earthly, thou a heavenly love;
  Thy grace being gained cures all disgrace in me.
Vows are but breath, and breath a vapor is; 70
  Then thou, fair sun, which on my earth dost shine,
Exhalest this vapor-vow; in thee it is.
  If broken then, it is no fault of mine;
If by me broke, what fool is not so wise
To lose an oath to win a paradise?" 75

Ber. This is the liver-vein, which makes flesh a deity,
A green goose a goddess—pure, pure idolatry.
God amend us, God amend! we are much out o' the way! 80

Enter Dumaine, [with a paper].

Long. By whom shall I send this?—Company! Stay! [*Steps aside.*]

Ber. "All hid, all hid"—an old infant play.
Like a demigod here sit I in the sky,
And wretched fools' secrets heedfully o'ereye.
More sacks to the mill! O heavens, I have my wish! 85
Dumaine transformed! Four woodcocks in a dish!

Dum. O most divine Kate!

Ber. O most profane coxcomb!

Dum. By heaven, the wonder in a mortal eye!

Ber. By earth, she is not, corporal: there you lie. 90

Dum. Her amber hair for foul hath amber quoted.

Ber. An amber-colored raven was well noted.

101. Is not that a good word: isn't it kind of me to say so.

105. Sweet misprision: amiable mistake.

110. passing: exceedingly.

Dum. As upright as the cedar.

Ber. Stoop, I say;

Her shoulder is with child. 95

Dum. As fair as day.

Ber. Ay, as some days; but then no sun must shine.

Dum. O that I had my wish!

Long. And I had mine!

King. And I mine too, good Lord! 100

Ber. Amen, so I had mine! Is not that a good word?

Dum. I would forget her; but a fever she
Reigns in my blood, and will rememb'red be.

Ber. A fever in your blood? Why, then, incision
Would let her out in saucers. Sweet misprision! 105

Dum. Once more I'll read the ode that I have writ.

Ber. Once more I'll mark how love can vary wit.

Dum. *Reads his sonnet.*

"On a day—alack the day!—
Love, whose month is ever May,
Spied a blossom passing fair 110
Playing in the wanton air.
Through the velvet leaves the wind,
All unseen, can passage find;
That the lover, sick to death,
Wished himself the heaven's breath. 115
'Air,' quoth he, 'thy cheeks may blow;
Air, would I might triumph so!
But, alack, my hand is sworn
Ne'er to pluck thee from thy thorn;
Vow, alack, for youth unmeet, 120
Youth so apt to pluck a sweet.
Do not call it sin in me

126. deny himself for Jove: deny he was Jove.

That I am forsworn for thee;
Thou for whom Jove would swear
Juno but an Ethiope were; 125
And deny himself for Jove,
Turning mortal for thy love.'"
This will I send; and something else more plain
That shall express my true love's fasting pain.
O, would the King, Berowne, and Longaville, 130
Were lovers too! Ill, to example ill,
Would from my forehead wipe a perjured note;
For none offend where all alike do dote.

Long. [*Advancing*] Dumaine, thy love is far from charity, 135
That in love's grief desirest society;
You may look pale, but I should blush, I know,
To be o'erheard and taken napping so.

King. [*Advancing*] Come, sir, you blush; as his, your case is such. 140
You chide at him, offending twice as much:
You do not love Maria! Longaville
Did never sonnet for her sake compile;
Nor never lay his wreathed arms athwart
His loving bosom to keep down his heart. 145
I have been closely shrouded in this bush,
And marked you both, and for you both did blush.
I heard your guilty rhymes, observed your fashion,
Saw sighs reek from you, noted well your passion.
"Ay me!" says one. "O Jove!" the other cries. 150
One, her hairs were gold; crystal the other's eyes.
[*To Longaville*] You would for paradise break faith and troth;

161. **by:** about.

176. **teen:** grief.

179. **gig:** top.

181. **Nestor:** one of the wisest of the Greek heroes; **pushpin:** a child's game.

182. **critic Timon:** a noted misanthrope of ancient Athens.

[*To Dumaine*] And Jove for your love would infringe an oath. 155
What will Berowne say when that he shall hear
Faith infringed which such zeal did swear?
How will he scorn, how will he spend his wit!
How will he triumph, leap, and laugh at it!
For all the wealth that ever I did see, 160
I would not have him know so much by me.

Ber. [*Advancing*] Now step I forth to whip hypocrisy.
Ah, good my liege, I pray thee pardon me.
Good heart, what grace hast thou thus to reprove 165
These worms for loving, that art most in love?
Your eyes do make no coaches; in your tears
There is no certain princess that appears;
You'll not be perjured; 'tis a hateful thing;
Tush, none but minstrels like of sonneting. 170
But are you not ashamed? Nay, are you not,
All three of you, to be thus much o'ershot?
You found his mote; the King your mote did see;
But I a beam do find in each of three.
O, what a scene of fool'ry have I seen, 175
Of sighs, of groans, of sorrow, and of teen!
O me, with what strict patience have I sat,
To see a king transformed to a gnat!
To see great Hercules whipping a gig,
And profound Solomon to tune a jig, 180
And Nestor play at pushpin with the boys,
And critic Timon laugh at idle toys!
Where lies thy grief, O, tell me, good Dumaine?
And, gentle Longaville, where lies thy pain?

186. **caudle:** a warm drink, usually containing spiced and sweetened ale or wine, used to comfort invalids.

193. **moon-like men:** George Steevens' suggestion. The Quarto and Folio read "men like men."

196. **pruning:** preening; primping (to win a woman's favor).

198. **state:** dignified bearing.

202. **post:** ride posthaste.

204. **present:** presentment.

211. **misdoubts:** suspects.

And where my liege's? All about the breast. 185
A caudle, ho!
King. Too bitter is thy jest.
Are we betrayed thus to thy overview?
Ber. Not you by me, but I betrayed to you.
I that am honest, I that hold it sin 190
To break the vow I am engaged in;
I am betrayed by keeping company
With moon-like men, men of inconstancy.
When shall you see me write a thing in rhyme?
Or groan for Joan? or spend a minute's time 195
In pruning me? When shall you hear that I
Will praise a hand, a foot, a face, an eye,
A gait, a state, a brow, a breast, a waist,
A leg, a limb—
King. Soft! whither away so fast? 200
A true man or a thief that gallops so?
Ber. I post from love; good lover, let me go.

Enter Jaquenetta and Costard.

Jaq. God bless the King!
King. What present hast thou there?
Cost. Some certain treason. 205
King. What makes treason here?
Cost. Nay, it makes nothing, sir.
King. If it mar nothing neither,
The treason and you go in peace away together.
Jaq. I beseech your Grace, let this letter be read; 210
Our person misdoubts it: 'twas treason, he said.

219. toy: trifle.

224. whoreson: good-for-nothing; **loggerhead:** blockhead.

229. the mess: i.e., a party of four, the usual grouping at meals where many guests were present.

231. pickpurses: pickpockets.

235. turtles: turtledoves.

King. Berowne, read it over.

He [Berowne] reads the letter.

Where hadst thou it?

Jaq. Of Costard.

King. Where hadst thou it? 215

Cost. Of Dun Adramadio, Dun Adramadio.

[Berowne tears the letter.]

King. How now! What is in you? Why dost thou tear it?

Ber. A toy, my liege, a toy! Your Grace needs not fear it. 220

Long. It did move him to passion, and therefore let's hear it.

Dum. It is Berowne's writing, and here is his name.

[Gathering up the pieces.]

Ber. *[To Costard]* Ah, you whoreson loggerhead, you were born to do me shame. 225

Guilty, my lord, guilty! I confess, I confess.

King. What?

Ber. That you three fools lacked me fool to make up the mess.

He, he, and you—and you, my liege!—and I 230

Are pickpurses in love, and we deserve to die.

O, dismiss this audience, and I shall tell you more.

Dum. Now the number is even.

Ber. True, true, we are four.

Will these turtles be gone? 235

King. Hence, sirs, away.

Cost. Walk aside the true folk, and let the traitors stay. *[Exeunt Costard and Jaquenetta.]*

Ber. Sweet lords, sweet lovers, O, let us embrace!

244. of all hands: on every side; no matter how you look at it.

245. rent: torn.

253. peremptory: commanding.

261. the culled sovereignty: the choicest and most excellent. **Culled** means "carefully selected."

263. several worthies make one dignity: various excellencies combine in an eminent whole. The total effect of her several points of beauty is a surpassing loveliness.

264. wants: lacks.

265. flourish: gift for florid description; **gentle:** cultivated.

268. praise too short doth blot: praise which is inadequate actually blemishes her.

As true we are as flesh and blood can be. 240
The sea will ebb and flow, heaven show his face;
Young blood doth not obey an old decree.
We cannot cross the cause why we were born,
Therefore of all hands must we be forsworn.

King. What, did these rent lines show some love of thine? 245

Ber. "Did they?" quoth you. Who sees the heavenly Rosaline
That, like a rude and savage man of Inde
At the first op'ning of the gorgeous east, 250
Bows not his vassal head and, strucken blind,
Kisses the base ground with obedient breast?
What peremptory eagle-sighted eye
Dares look upon the heaven of her brow
That is not blinded by her majesty? 255

King. What zeal, what fury hath inspired thee now?
My love, her mistress, is a gracious moon;
She, an attending star, scarce seen a light.

Ber. My eyes are then no eyes, nor I Berowne.
O, but for my love, day would turn to night! 260
Of all complexions the culled sovereignty
Do meet, as at a fair, in her fair cheek,
Where several worthies make one dignity,
Where nothing wants that want itself doth seek.
Lend me the flourish of all gentle tongues— 265
Fie, painted rhetoric! O, she needs it not!
To things of sale a seller's praise belongs:
She passes praise; then praise too short doth blot.
A withered hermit, fivescore winters worn,
Might shake off fifty, looking in her eye. 270

274. **black as ebony:** to the Elizabethan taste, fairness was a requisite of beauty.

283. **beauty's crest becomes the heavens well:** i.e., in contrast to **black,** which is the **badge of hell.** It is paradoxical, therefore, that the black (brunette) Rosaline should be considered the model of beauty.

287-88. **mourns that painting and usurping hair/Should ravish doters with a false aspect:** i.e., her countenance is dark with dismay that beauty dependent on paint and false hair should be admired.

290. **favor:** face, with special reference to her complexion.

295. **colliers:** dealers in coal.

298. **crack:** brag.

Beauty doth varnish age, as if newborn,
And gives the crutch the cradle's infancy.
O, 'tis the sun that maketh all things shine!
King. By heaven, thy love is black as ebony.
Ber. Is ebony like her? O, wood divine! 275
A wife of such wood were felicity.
O, who can give an oath? Where is a book?
That I may swear beauty doth beauty lack,
If that she learn not of her eye to look.
No face is fair that is not full so black. 280
King. O paradox! Black is the badge of hell,
The hue of dungeons, and the school of night;
And beauty's crest becomes the heavens well.
Ber. Devils soonest tempt, resembling spirits of light. 285
O, if in black my lady's brows be decked,
It mourns that painting and usurping hair
Should ravish doters with a false aspect;
And therefore is she born to make black fair.
Her favor turns the fashion of the days; 290
For native blood is counted painting now;
And therefore red that would avoid dispraise
Paints itself black, to imitate her brow.
Dum. To look like her are chimney sweepers black.
Long. And since her time are colliers counted bright. 295
King. And Ethiopes of their sweet complexion crack.
Dum. Dark needs no candles now, for dark is light.
Ber. Your mistresses dare never come in rain 300
For fear their colors should be washed away.

321. **quillets:** quibbles; clever dodges.

330-51. **And . . . there:** the italicized passage contains phraseology that is partly repeated beginning at l. 352 and suggests a partial rewriting without deletion of the earlier draft. Since it is impossible to decide what the author intended, all of the lines are printed.

King. 'Twere good yours did; for, sir, to tell you plain,
I'll find a fairer face not washed today.
Ber. I'll prove her fair, or talk till doomsday here. 305
King. No devil will fright thee then so much as she.
Dum. I never knew man hold vile stuff so dear.
Long. Look, here's thy love: my foot and her face see. [*Showing his shoe.*]
Ber. O, if the streets were paved with thine eyes, 310
Her feet were much too dainty for such tread!
Dum. O vile! Then, as she goes, what upward lies
The street should see as she walked overhead.
King. But what of this? Are we not all in love?
Ber. Nothing so sure; and thereby all forsworn. 315
King. Then leave this chat; and, good Berowne, now prove
Our loving lawful, and our faith not torn.
Dum. Ay, marry, there; some flattery for this evil.
Long. O, some authority how to proceed; 320
Some tricks, some quillets, how to cheat the devil!
Dum. Some salve for perjury.
Ber. 'Tis more than need.
Have at you, then, affection's men-at-arms!
Consider what you first did swear unto: 325
To fast, to study, and to see no woman—
Flat treason 'gainst the kingly state of youth.
Say, can you fast? Your stomachs are too young,
And abstinence engenders maladies.

And where that you have vowed to study, lords, 330
In that each of you have forsworn his book,

338. **Promethean fire:** creative inspiration.
356. **fiery numbers:** passionate verses.
358. **keep:** keep to; abide within.

Can you still dream, and pore, and thereon look?
For when would you, my lord, or you, or you,
Have found the ground of study's excellence
Without the beauty of a woman's face? 335
From women's eyes this doctrine I derive:
They are the ground, the books, the academes,
From whence doth spring the true Promethean fire.
Why, universal plodding poisons up
The nimble spirits in the arteries, 340
As motion and long-during action tires
The sinewy vigor of the traveler.
Now, for not looking on a woman's face,
You have in that forsworn the use of eyes,
And study too, the causer of your vow; 345
For where is any author in the world
Teaches such beauty as a woman's eye?
Learning is but an adjunct to ourself,
And where we are our learning likewise is;
Then, when ourselves we see in ladies' eyes, 350
Do we not likewise see our learning there?

O, we have made a vow to study, lords,
And in that vow we have forsworn our books.
For when would you, my liege, or you, or you,
In leaden contemplation have found out 355
Such fiery numbers as the prompting eyes
Of beauty's tutors have enriched you with?
Other slow arts entirely keep the brain;
And therefore, finding barren practicers,
Scarce show a harvest of their heavy toil; 360
But love, first learned in a lady's eyes,

370. **When the suspicious head of theft is stopped:** i.e., the lover can hear sounds inaudible even to the wary thief.

371. **sensible:** sensitive.

375. **climbing trees in the Hesperides:** Hercules' twelfth labor was to bring back the golden apples from the Garden of the Hesperides.

Bright Apollo. From Giulio Cesare Capaccio, *Gli apologi* (1619)

Lives not alone immured in the brain,
But with the motion of all elements
Courses as swift as thought in every power,
And gives to every power a double power, 365
Above their functions and their offices.
It adds a precious seeing to the eye:
A lover's eyes will gaze an eagle blind.
A lover's ear will hear the lowest sound,
When the suspicious head of theft is stopped. 370
Love's feeling is more soft and sensible
Than are the tender horns of cockled snails.
Love's tongue proves dainty Bacchus gross in taste.
For valor, is not Love a Hercules,
Still climbing trees in the Hesperides? 375
Subtle as Sphinx; as sweet and musical
As bright Apollo's lute, strung with his hair.
And when Love speaks, the voice of all the gods
Make heaven drowsy with the harmony.
Never durst poet touch a pen to write 380
Until his ink were temp'red with Love's sighs;
O, then his lines would ravish savage ears,
And plant in tyrants mild humility.
From women's eyes this doctrine I derive:
They sparkle still the right Promethean fire; 385
They are the books, the arts, the academes,
That show, contain, and nourish all the world,
Else none at all in aught proves excellent.
Then fools you were these women to forswear;
Or, keeping what is sworn, you will prove fools. 390
For wisdom's sake, a word that all men love;
Or for Love's sake, a word that loves all men;

398. charity itself fulfills the law: a reference to Rom. 13:8 and 10.

401. Advance your standards: raise your flags.

402. be . . . advised: take care.

403. get the sun of: secure the advantage over.

404. Now to plain dealing; lay these glozes by: let's talk plainly; put aside these metaphors.

410. attach: seize.

416. time: opportunity.

417. betime: chance.

418. cockle: a weed which grows in cornfields.

Or for men's sake, the authors of these women;
Or women's sake, by whom we men are men—
Let us once lose our oaths to find ourselves, 395
Or else we lose ourselves to keep our oaths.
It is religion to be thus forsworn;
For charity itself fulfills the law,
And who can sever love from charity?

King. Saint Cupid, then! and, soldiers, to the field! 400

Ber. Advance your standards, and upon them, lords!
Pell-mell, down with them! But be first advised,
In conflict, that you get the sun of them.

Long. Now to plain dealing; lay these glozes by.
Shall we resolve to woo these girls of France? 405

King. And win them too; therefore let us devise
Some entertainment for them in their tents.

Ber. First, from the park let us conduct them thither;
Then homeward every man attach the hand 410
Of his fair mistress. In the afternoon
We will with some strange pastime solace them,
Such as the shortness of the time can shape;
For revels, dances, masks, and merry hours
Forerun fair Love, strewing her way with flowers. 415

King. Away, away! No time shall be omitted
That will betime, and may by us be fitted.

Ber. Allons! allons! Sowed cockle reaped no corn,
And justice always whirls in equal measure.
Light wenches may prove plagues to men forsworn; 420
If so, our copper buys no better treasure.

Exeunt.

Or for men's sake, the authors of these women;
Or women's sake, by whom we men are men—
Let us once lose our oaths to find ourselves, 395
Or else we lose ourselves to keep our oaths.
It is religion to be thus forsworn;
For charity itself fulfils the law;
And who can sever love from charity?

King. Saint Cupid, then! and, soldiers, to the field! 400

Ber. Advance your standards, and upon them, lords!
Pell-mell, down with them! But be first advised,
In conflict, that you get the sun of them.

Long. Now to plain dealing; lay these glozes by.
Shall we resolve to woo these girls of France? 405

King. And win them too; therefore let us devise
Some entertainment for them in their tents.

Ber. First, from the park let us conduct them thither;
Then homeward every man attach the hand 410
Of his fair mistress. In the afternoon
We will with some strange pastime solace them,
Such as the shortness of the time can shape;
For revels, dances, masks, and merry hours
Forerun fair Love, strewing her way with flowers. 415

King. Away, away! No time shall be omitted
That will betime, and may by us be fitted.

Ber. Allons! allons! Sowed cockle reaped no corn,
And justice always whirls in equal measure.
Light wenches may prove plagues to men forsworn; 420
If so, our copper buys no better treasure.

Exeunt.

LOVE'S LABOR'S LOST

ACT V

[V.i.] Armado reveals to Holofernes, Sir Nathaniel, Dull, Moth, and Costard that the King has asked him to prepare an entertainment for the ladies from France, and he proposes that they help him present the Nine Worthies.

1. **Satis quod sufficit:** enough is as good as a feast.

2. **reasons:** conversation.

3-4. **sententious:** wise and meaningful; **pleasant without scurrility:** facetious without indecency; **affection:** affectation; **audacious:** confident.

5. **opinion:** self-conceit.

6-7. **this quondam day:** yesterday.

9. **Novi hominem tanquam te:** I know the man as well as I know you.

10. **filed:** polished; cultivated.

12. **thrasonical:** boastful; an adjective deriving from the vainglorious Thraso in Terence's *Eunuchus*.

13. **picked:** finical; overfastidious; **spruce:** dapper.

14. **peregrinate:** foreign-fashioned; characterized by foreign ways picked up in travel abroad.

S.D. after l. 15: **table book:** memorandum book or notebook.

16-7. **draweth out the thread of his verbosity finer than the staple of his argument:** talks at great length about little.

18-9. **fanatical:** excessive; extravagant; **insociable:** incompatible; impossible to get along with; **point-device:** precise or particular.

ACT V

[Scene I. The same.]

Enter Holofernes, Sir Nathaniel, and Dull.

Hol. Satis quod sufficit.

Nath. I praise God for you, sir. Your reasons at dinner have been sharp and sententious; pleasant without scurrility, witty without affection, audacious without impudency, learned without opinion, and strange without heresy. I did converse this quondam day with a companion of the King's who is intituled, nominated, or called, Don Adriano de Armado.

Hol. Novi hominem tanquam te. His humor is lofty, his discourse peremptory, his tongue filed, his eye ambitious, his gait majestical and his general behavior vain, ridiculous, and thrasonical. He is too picked, too spruce, too affected, too odd, as it were, too peregrinate, as I may call it.

Nath. A most singular and choice epithet.

Draws out his table book.

Hol. He draweth out the thread of his verbosity finer than the staple of his argument. I abhor such fanatical phantasimes, such insociable and point-device companions; such rackers of orthography, as

22. **clepeth:** calls.

23. **vocatur:** is called.

24. **abhominable:** by mistaken etymology contemporary scholars derived the word from *ab homine* instead of *ab omine*. Holofernes would have the *h* pronounced.

25-6. **It insinuateth me of insanie:** i.e., to me it seems utter madness; **ne intelligis, domine:** do you understand, sir.

27. **Laus Deo, bene intelligo:** praise God, I understand well.

28. **Bon, bon, fort bon:** good, good, very good. This is the plausible correction suggested by the Cambridge editors, Professors Clark and Wright, for the garbled "Bome boon for boon" in the early texts; **Priscian:** a Latin grammarian whose texts were well-known.

30. **Videsne quis venit:** do you see who comes.

31. **Video, et gaudeo:** I see and rejoice.

32. **Chirrah:** Sirrah. The spelling reflects Armado's pronunciation.

33. **Quare:** why.

38. **alms basket:** the scraps collected as alms for the poor; leftovers.

41. **honorificabilitudinitatibus:** from the medieval Latin *honorificabilitudo* (honorableness). Generally credited with being the longest word known.

42. **flapdragon:** a flaming raisin. A party game similar to ducking for apples consisted of snapping for such tidbits in a bowl of burning brandy.

46. **hornbook:** children learned their ABC's from alphabets pasted on paddles of wood covered with horn.

to speak "dout" fine, when he should say "doubt"; "det" when he should pronounce "debt"—d, e, b, t, not d, e, t. He clepeth a calf "cauf," half "hauf"; neighbor *vocatur* "nebor"; neigh abbreviated "ne." This is abhominable—which he would call "abbominable." It insinuateth me of insanie: *ne intelligis, domine?* to make frantic, lunatic.

Nath. *Laus Deo, bene intelligo.*

Hol. *Bon, bon, fort bon!* Priscian a little scratched; 'twill serve.

Enter Armado, Moth, and Costard.

Nath. *Videsne quis venit?*

Hol. *Video, et gaudeo.*

Arm. [*To Moth*] Chirrah!

Hol. *Quare* "chirrah," not "sirrah"?

Arm. Men of peace, well encount'red.

Hol. Most military sir, salutation.

Moth. [*Aside to Costard*] They have been at a great feast of languages and stol'n the scraps.

Cost. O, they have lived long on the alms basket of words. I marvel thy master hath not eaten thee for a word, for thou art not so long by the head as honorificabilitudinitatibus; thou art easier swallowed than a flapdragon.

Moth. Peace! the peal begins.

Arm. [*To Holofernes*] Monsieur, are you not lettered?

Moth. Yes, yes; he teaches boys the hornbook.

49. **pueritia:** child.

52. **Quis:** what; **consonant:** nonentity (because it requires a vowel to be sounded).

57. **Mediterraneum:** a contemporary spelling of "Mediterranean."

58. **venue:** sally.

61. **wit-old:** i.e., wittol; a word meaning both half-wit and cuckold.

62. **figure:** metaphor.

66. **circum circa:** round and about. This is Lewis Theobald's suggestion for the meaningless "unum cita" which appears in the early texts.

76. **unguem:** the correct phrase would be *ad unguem:* to the nail.

77. **Artsman:** master of arts; scholar; **preambulate:** go before; precede me.

A cuckold. From a seventeenth-century ballad.

What is a, b, spelt backward with the horn on his head?

Hol. Ba, *pueritia*, with a horn added.

Moth. Ba, most silly sheep with a horn. You hear his learning. 50

Hol. *Quis*, *quis*, thou consonant?

Moth. The third of the five vowels, if you repeat them; or the fifth, if I.

Hol. I will repeat them: a, e, I— 55

Moth. The sheep; the other two concludes it: o, U.

Arm. Now, by the salt wave of the Mediterraneum, a sweet touch, a quick venue of wit!—snip, snap, quick and home. It rejoiceth my intellect. True wit!

Moth. Offered by a child to an old man; which is wit-old. 60

Hol. What is the figure? What is the figure?

Moth. Horns!

Hol. Thou disputes like an infant; go whip thy gig.

Moth. Lend me your horn to make one, and I will whip about your infamy *circum circa*—a gig of a cuckold's horn. 65

Cost. An I had but one penny in the world, thou shouldst have it to buy gingerbread. Hold, there is the very remuneration I had of thy master, thou halfpenny purse of wit, thou pigeon egg of discretion. O, an the heavens were so pleased that thou wert but my bastard, what a joyful father wouldst thou make me! Go to; thou hast it *ad dunghill*, at the fingers' ends, as they say. 70 75

Hol. O, I smell false Latin: *dunghill* for *unguem*.

Arm. Artsman, preambulate; we will be singled

78-9. **the charge house on the top of the mountain:** an allusion to a satirical passage in Erasmus' *Colloquies*, familiar to schoolboys. See the comment in R. David's edition of *Love's Labor's Lost* in the Arden series (London, 1951), p. 126.

84. **affection:** inclination; **congratulate:** salute; show a courteous welcome to.

88. **liable:** suitable.

94. **remember thy courtesy:** it was courtesy to remove the hat when greeting a friend, in presence of the King, and even at the mention of the King's name. Armado is reminding Holofernes that he may now put his hat back on. See *Hamlet*, V. ii. 101-11.

95. **importunate:** pressing.

99-100. **excrement:** outgrowth (of hair).

108. **antic:** bit of foolery.

from the barbarous. Do you not educate youth at the charge house on the top of the mountain?

Hol. Or *mons*, the hill. 80

Arm. At your sweet pleasure, for the mountain.

Hol. I do, sans question.

Arm. Sir, it is the King's most sweet pleasure and affection to congratulate the Princess at her pavilion in the posteriors of this day, which the rude multitude call the afternoon. 85

Hol. The posterior of the day, most generous sir, is liable, congruent, and measurable for the afternoon. The word is well culled, chose; sweet, and apt, I do assure you, sir, I do assure. 90

Arm. Sir, the King is a noble gentleman, and my familiar, I do assure ye, very good friend. For what is inward between us, let it pass. I do beseech thee, remember thy courtesy. I beseech thee, apparel thy head. And among other importunate and most serious designs, and of great import indeed, too—but let that pass; for I must tell thee it will please his Grace, by the world! sometime to lean upon my poor shoulder, and with his royal finger thus dally with my excrement, with my mustachio; but, sweet heart, let that pass. By the world, I recount no fable: some certain special honors it pleaseth his greatness to impart to Armado, a soldier, a man of travel, that hath seen the world; but let that pass. The very all of all is—but, sweet heart, I do implore secrecy—that the King would have me present the Princess, sweet chuck, with some delightful ostentation, or show, or pageant, or antic, or firework. Now, understanding that the

113-14. the Nine Worthies: usually given as Hector, Alexander, Julius Cæsar, Joshua, David, Judas Maccabæus, Arthur, Charlemagne, and either Guy of Warwick or Godfrey of Bouillon, but this list was not invariable.

129. Shall I have audience: will you hear me out.

131. strangling a snake: the infant Hercules strangled with his bare hands two snakes sent by Juno to kill him.

Joshua, one of the Nine Worthies. Guillaume Rouillé, *Promptuarii iconum* (1553)

curate and your sweet self are good at such eruptions and sudden breaking-out of mirth, as it were, I have 110 acquainted you withal, to the end to crave your assistance.

Hol. Sir, you shall present before her the Nine Worthies. Sir Nathaniel, as concerning some entertainment of time, some show in the posterior of this 115 day, to be rend'red by our assistance, the King's command, and this most gallant, illustrate, and learned gentleman, before the Princess—I say none so fit as to present the Nine Worthies.

Nath. Where will you find men worthy enough to 120 present them?

Hol. Joshua, yourself; myself; this gallant gentleman, Judas Maccabæus; this swain, because of his great limb or joint, shall pass Pompey the Great; the page, Hercules. 125

Arm. Pardon, sir; error: he is not quantity enough for that Worthy's thumb; he is not so big as the end of his club.

Hol. Shall I have audience? He shall present Hercules in minority: his enter and exit shall be 130 strangling a snake; and I will have an apology for that purpose.

Moth. An excellent device! So, if any of the audience hiss, you may cry, "Well done, Hercules; now thou crushest the snake!" That is the way to 135 make an offense gracious, though few have the grace to do it.

Arm. For the rest of the Worthies?

Hol. I will play three myself.

143. **fadge:** pass; succeed.

145. **Via:** "Come, join in; what say you?" An Italian word used to encourage or prompt a horse.

149. **so:** something of that sort.

150. **tabor:** little drum.

151. **hay:** a country dance similar to a reel.

[V.ii.] The ladies have all received love tokens from their respective suitors and resolve to be merry at their expense. Boyet reports that the King and his lords are coming to woo them in the guise of Russians. All mask themselves and exchange their tokens so that each man will court the wrong lady. The unhappy lords are bested by the ladies' wit but shortly return in their rightful guise to try again. Berowne soon suspects that Boyet had forewarned the ladies of their identities.

Armado and his company, with their presentation of the Nine Worthies, give the lords an opportunity to exercise their own wits. The fun is interrupted, however, by the appearance of Marcade, a messenger from France, with the news that the Princess' father is dead. An immediate return to France is necessary and the time is too short for the skeptical women to be convinced of the sincerity of their lovers. They promise to give their answers in a year's time and suggest that a favorable reply may be won if the men will lead lives of austerity and usefulness in the meantime.

---

2. **fairings:** gifts.

10. **wax:** grow; with a pun referring to **seal** in the previous line.

Moth. Thrice-worthy gentleman! 140

Arm. Shall I tell you a thing?

Hol. We attend.

Arm. We will have, if this fadge not, an antic. I beseech you, follow.

Hol. Via, goodman Dull! Thou has spoken no word 145 all this while.

Dull. Nor understood none neither, sir.

Hol. Allons! we will employ thee.

Dull. I'll make one in a dance, or so, or I will play
On the tabor to the Worthies, and let them dance the 150
hay.

Hol. Most dull, honest Dull! To our sport, away!
Exeunt.

[Scene II. The same.]

Enter the Princess, Maria, Katharine, and Rosaline.

Prin. Sweet hearts, we shall be rich ere we depart,
If fairings come thus plentifully in.
A lady walled about with diamonds!
Look you what I have from the loving King.

Ros. Madam, came nothing else along with that? 5

Prin. Nothing but this! Yes, as much love in rhyme
As would be crammed up in a sheet of paper
Writ o' both sides the leaf, margent and all,
That he was fain to seal on Cupid's name.

Ros. That was the way to make his godhead wax; 10
For he hath been five thousand year a boy.

12. **shrewd:** malicious; evil; **unhappy:** unlucky; **gallows:** rogue.

15. **melancholy, sad . . . heavy:** synonymous.

16. **light:** both "lighthearted" and "light in behavior" are meant.

24. **taking it in snuff:** i.e., resenting her words.

26. **still:** always.

28. **weigh:** match in weight, and value or esteem.

31. **past cure is still past care:** proverbial.

33. **favor:** token from a suitor, but Rosaline pretends that her face is meant.

39. **numbering:** explained by l. 41; i.e., accounting of my beauty.

41. **fairs:** beauties.

Kath. Ay, and a shrewd unhappy gallows too.
Ros. You'll ne'er be friends with him: 'a killed your sister.
Kath. He made her melancholy, sad, and heavy; 15
And so she died. Had she been light, like you,
Of such a merry, nimble, stirring spirit,
She might 'a been a grandam ere she died.
And so may you; for a light heart lives long.
Ros. What's your dark meaning, mouse, of this light word? 20
Kath. A light condition in a beauty dark.
Ros. We need more light to find your meaning out.
Kath. You'll mar the light by taking it in snuff;
Therefore I'll darkly end the argument. 25
Ros. Look what you do, you do it still i' the dark.
Kath. So do not you; for you are a light wench.
Ros. Indeed, I weigh not you; and therefore light.
Kath. You weigh me not? O, that's you care not for me. 30
Ros. Great reason; for "past cure is still past care."
Prin. Well bandied both; a set of wit well played.
But, Rosaline, you have a favor too?
Who sent it? and what is it?
Ros. I would you knew. 35
An if my face were but as fair as yours,
My favor were as great: be witness this.
Nay, I have verses too, I thank Berowne;
The numbers true, and, were the numbering too,
I were the fairest goddess on the ground. 40
I am compared to twenty thousand fairs.
O, he hath drawn my picture in his letter!

44. **Much in the letters; nothing in the praise:** i.e., the writing is fair, although the praise is inaccurate.

45. **ink:** another gibe at Rosaline's dark coloring, as is l. 46.

47. **Ware pencils:** you should beware of pencils (small brushes used by painters). Rosaline means either that Katharine already does too much touching up of her complexion, or that her complexion is so spotty that it needs retouching; **Let me not die your debtor:** i.e., I must repay the insult you have paid me.

48. **red dominical:** the letter D for Sunday, *dies dominica*. Rosaline also calls Katharine a **golden letter** because the dominical is precious and Katharine has golden hair. The implication is that her coloring is artificial.

49. **oes:** rounds; i.e., spots or pockmarks.

50. **beshrew all shrows:** literally, curse all shrews. The Princess has had enough of this exchange of insults.

67. **in by the week:** permanently caught; a phrase of unknown origin.

70. **bootless:** unavailing.

71. **hests:** commands.

72. **make him proud to make me proud that jests:** dress himself in finery to do honor to me when I am only having fun with him.

Prin. Anything like?
Ros. Much in the letters; nothing in the praise.
Prin. Beauteous as ink—a good conclusion. 45
Kath. Fair as a text B in a copybook.
Ros. Ware pencils, ho! Let me not die your debtor,
My red dominical, my golden letter.
O that your face were not so full of oes!
Prin. A pox of that jest! and I beshrew all shrows! 50
But, Katharine, what was sent to you from fair
Dumaine?
Kath. Madam, this glove.
Prin. Did he not send you twain?
Kath. Yes, madam; and moreover, 55
Some thousand verses of a faithful lover;
A huge translation of hypocrisy,
Vilely compiled, profound simplicity.
Mar. This, and these pearls to me sent Longaville;
The letter is too long by half a mile. 60
Prin. I think no less. Dost thou not wish in heart
The chain were longer and the letter short?
Mar. Ay, or I would these hands might never part.
Prin. We are wise girls to mock our lovers so.
Ros. They are worse fools to purchase mocking so. 65
That same Berowne I'll torture ere I go.
O that I knew he were but in by the week!
How I would make him fawn, and beg, and seek,
And wait the season, and observe the times,
And spend his prodigal wits in bootless rhymes, 70
And shape his service wholly to my hests,
And make him proud to make me proud that jests!

73. **pair-taunt:** a term from the card game "Post and Pair," meaning a combination of cards that beats others.

77-9. **folly, in wisdom hatched,/Hath wisdom's warrant and the help of school,/And wit's own grace to grace a learned fool:** when an intelligent person turns foolish, his very advantages of intelligence, schooling, and wit guarantee that he will excel at being a fool.

81. **wantonness:** frivolity.

93. **surprised:** captured.

96. **Saint Denis:** the patron saint of France.

97. **charge their breath:** prime themselves to win us with words.

So pair-taunt-like would I o'ersway his state
That he should be my fool, and I his fate.
Prin. None are so surely caught, when they are catched, 75
As wit turned fool; folly, in wisdom hatched,
Hath wisdom's warrant and the help of school,
And wit's own grace to grace a learned fool.
Ros. The blood of youth burns not with such excess 80
As gravity's revolt to wantonness.
Mar. Folly in fools bears not so strong a note
As fool'ry in the wise when wit doth dote,
Since all the power thereof it doth apply
To prove, by wit, worth in simplicity. 85

Enter Boyet.

Prin. Here comes Boyet, and mirth is in his face.
Boy. O, I am stabbed with laughter! Where's her Grace?
Prin. Thy news, Boyet?
Boy. Prepare, madam, prepare! 90
Arm, wenches, arm! Encounters mounted are
Against your peace. Love doth approach disguised,
Armed in arguments; you'll be surprised.
Muster your wits; stand in your own defense;
Or hide your heads like cowards and fly hence. 95
Prin. Saint Denis to Saint Cupid! What are they
That charge their breath against us? Say, scout, say.
Boy. Under the cool shade of a sycamore
I thought to close mine eyes some half an hour;
When, lo! to interrupt my purposed rest, 100

101. **addressed:** directed; moving in the direction of.

111. **Presence majestical would put him out:** such an august presence would cause him to forget his lines.

119. **fleered:** grinned.

121. **with his finger and his thumb:** i.e., snapping his fingers.

127-28. **in this spleen ridiculous appears,/To check their folly, passion's solemn tears:** i.e., they laughed until they cried.

A sixteenth-century Russian. From Cesare Vecellio, *Habiti antichi et moderni di tutto il mondo* (1598)

Toward that shade I might behold addressed
The King and his companions; warily
I stole into a neighbor thicket by,
And overheard what you shall overhear:
That, by and by, disguised they will be here. 105
Their herald is a pretty knavish page,
That well by heart hath conned his embassage.
Action and accent did they teach him there:
"Thus must thou speak and thus thy body bear,"
And ever and anon they made a doubt 110
Presence majestical would put him out;
"For," quoth the King, "an angel shalt thou see;
Yet fear not thou, but speak audaciously."
The boy replied, "An angel is not evil;
I should have feared her had she been a devil." 115
With that all laughed, and clapped him on the shoulder,
Making the bold wag by their praises bolder.
One rubbed his elbow, thus, and fleered, and swore
A better speech was never spoke before. 120
Another with his finger and his thumb
Cried, "Via! we will do't, come what will come."
The third he capered, and cried, "All goes well."
The fourth turned on the toe, and down he fell.
With that they all did tumble on the ground, 125
With such a zealous laughter, so profound,
That in this spleen ridiculous appears,
To check their folly, passion's solemn tears.

Prin. But what, but what, come they to visit us?

Boy. They do, they do, and are appareled thus, 130
Like Muscovites or Russians, as I guess.

137. **tasked:** hard put to it.

139. **grace:** good fortune or privilege.

147. **most in sight:** where they cannot fail to be seen.

158. **grace:** favor.

Their purpose is to parley, court, and dance;
And every one his love feat will advance
Unto his several mistress; which they'll know
By favors several which they did bestow. 135

Prin. And will they so? The gallants shall be tasked,
For, ladies, we will every one be masked,
And not a man of them shall have the grace,
Despite of suit, to see a lady's face. 140
Hold, Rosaline, this favor thou shalt wear,
And then the King will court thee for his dear;
Hold, take thou this, my sweet, and give me thine,
So shall Berowne take me for Rosaline.
And change you favors too; so shall your loves 145
Woo contrary, deceived by these removes.

Ros. Come on, then, wear the favors most in sight.

Kath. But, in this changing, what is your intent?

Prin. The effect of my intent is to cross theirs.
They do it but in mocking merriment, 150
And mock for mock is only my intent.
Their several counsels they unbosom shall
To loves mistook, and so be mocked withal
Upon the next occasion that we meet,
With visages displayed, to talk and greet. 155

Ros. But shall we dance, if they desire us to't?

Prin. No, to the death, we will not move a foot,
Nor to their penned speech render we no grace;
But while 'tis spoke each turn away her face.

Boy. Why, that contempt will kill the speaker's heart, 160
And quite divorce his memory from his part.

172. **no richer than rich taffeta:** the taffeta of the ladies' masks is the only beauty visible about them.

Prin. Therefore I do it; and I make no doubt
The rest will ne'er come in, if he be out.
There's no such sport as sport by sport o'erthrown, 165
To make theirs ours, and ours none but our own;
So shall we stay, mocking intended game,
And they well mocked depart away with shame.
Sound trumpet [within].
Boy. The trumpet sounds; be masked; the maskers
come. *[The Ladies mask.]* 170

Enter Blackamoors with music, Moth with a speech, and the rest of the Lords, disguised [as Russians].

Moth. "All hail, the richest beauties on the earth!"
Boy. Beauties no richer than rich taffeta.
Moth. "A holy parcel of the fairest dames
The Ladies turn their backs to him.
That ever turned their—backs—to mortal views!"
Ber. "Their eyes," villain, "their eyes." 175
Moth. "That ever turned their eyes to mortal views!
Out—"
Boy. True; "out" indeed.
Moth. "Out of your favors, heavenly spirits, vouch-
safe 180
Not to behold—"
Ber. "Once to behold," rogue.
Moth. "Once to behold with your sun-beamed eyes
—with your sun-beamed eyes—"
Boy. They will not answer to that epithet; 185
You were best call it "daughter-beamed eyes."

203. tread a measure: dance a stately dance.

Moth. They do not mark me, and that brings me out.

Ber. Is this your perfectness? Be gone, you rogue.

[*Exit Moth.*]

Ros. What would these strangers? Know their minds, Boyet. 190

If they do speak our language, 'tis our will
That some plain man recount their purposes.
Know what they would.

Boy. What would you with the Princess? 195

Ber. Nothing but peace and gentle visitation.

Ros. What would they, say they?

Boy. Nothing but peace and gentle visitation.

Ros. Why, that they have; and bid them so be gone. 200

Boy. She says you have it, and you may be gone.

King. Say to her we have measured many miles
To tread a measure with her on this grass.

Boy. They say that they have measured many a mile 205
To tread a measure with you on this grass.

Ros. It is not so. Ask them how many inches
Is in one mile? If they have measured many,
The measure, then, of one is easily told.

Boy. If to come hither you have measured miles, 210
And many miles, the Princess bids you tell
How many inches doth fill up one mile.

Ber. Tell her we measure them by weary steps.

Boy. She hears herself.

Ros. How many weary steps 215

223. My face is but a moon, and clouded too: Rosaline means that she is not the luminary the King believes her to be, but one who reflects the Princess' brightness; also that she is not "fair" of face, and that her face is masked in addition.

224. do as such clouds do: i.e., kiss her face.

226. eyne: eyes.

230. change: i.e., dance, or round of a dance.

244. nice: punctilious about formalities.

Beginning of a dance. From Jehan Tabourot, *Orchesography* (1925 reprint)

Of many weary miles you have o'ergone
Are numb'red in the travail of one mile?
Ber. We number nothing that we spend for you;
Our duty is so rich, so infinite,
That we may do it still without account. 220
Vouchsafe to show the sunshine of your face,
That we, like savages, may worship it.
Ros. My face is but a moon, and clouded too.
King. Blessed are clouds, to do as such clouds do.
Vouchsafe, bright moon, and these thy stars, to shine, 225
Those clouds removed, upon our watery eyne.
Ros. O vain petitioner! beg a greater matter;
Thou now requests but moonshine in the water.
King. Then in our measure do but vouchsafe one change. 230
Thou bidst me beg; this begging is not strange.
Ros. Play music then. Nay, you must do it soon.
Not yet? No dance! Thus change I like the moon.
King. Will you not dance? How come you thus estranged? 235
Ros. You took the moon at full, but now she's changed.
King. Yet still she is the moon, and I the man.
The music plays; vouchsafe some motion to it.
Ros. Our ears vouchsafe it. 240
King. But your legs should do it.
Ros. Since you are strangers, and come here by chance,
We'll not be nice; take hands. We will not dance.
King. Why take we hands then? 245

248. More measure: that is, a kiss. A dance began with the exchange of bows, a handclasp, and then a kiss.

255. visor: mask.

262. two treys: two groups of three; the trey is the die with three spots; **nice:** literal; precise.

263. Metheglin: mead, a spiced drink made from fermented honey; **wort:** an infusion of malt or grain which was fermented to make beer or other spirits; **malmsey:** a sweet wine.

266. cog: cheat.

269. grievest my gall: hit me in a sore spot, and embitter me.

271. meet: suitable (in view of your bitter words).

272. change: exchange.

Ros. Only to part friends.
Curtsy, sweet hearts; and so the measure ends.
King. More measure of this measure; be not nice.
Ros. We can afford no more at such a price.
King. Price you yourselves. What buys your company? 250
Ros. Your absence only.
King. That can never be.
Ros. Then cannot we be bought; and so adieu—
Twice to your visor and half once to you! 255
King. If you deny to dance, let's hold more chat.
Ros. In private then.
King. I am best pleased with that.
[*They converse apart.*]
Ber. White-handed mistress, one sweet word with thee. 260
Prin. Honey, and milk, and sugar; there is three.
Ber. Nay, then, two treys, an if you grow so nice,
Metheglin, wort, and malmsey; well run dice!
There's half a dozen sweets.
Prin. Seventh sweet, adieu! 265
Since you can cog, I'll play no more with you.
Ber. One word in secret.
Prin. Let it not be sweet.
Ber. Thou grievest my gall.
Prin. Gall! bitter. 270
Ber. Therefore meet.
[*They converse apart.*]
Dum. Will you vouchsafe with me to change a word?

280. **vizard:** visor.

284. **a double tongue:** i.e., her own (which is prone to equivocal speech), and the tongue of the mask, a projection that was held in the mouth to keep the mask in place.

286. **"Veal," quoth the Dutchman:** "Well," as a Dutchman would pronounce it. **Veal** is also a common spelling of the time for "veil" (mask) and a phonetic spelling of the last syllable of Longaville's name, the first syllable of which had been Katharine's last word.

290. **part:** share.

291. **half:** i.e., better half; wife.

292. **ox:** fool.

302. **Above the sense of sense:** beyond ordinary comprehension; **sensible:** sensitive.

Mar. Name it.

Dum. Fair lady— 275

Mar. Say you so? Fair lord—

Take that for your fair lady.

Dum. Please it you,

As much in private, and I'll bid adieu.

[*They converse apart.*]

Kath. What, was your vizard made without a tongue? 280

Long. I know the reason, lady, why you ask.

Kath. O for your reason! Quickly, sir; I long.

Long. You have a double tongue within your mask,

And would afford my speechless vizard half. 285

Kath. "Veal," quoth the Dutchman. Is not "veal" a calf?

Long. A calf, fair lady!

Kath. No, a fair lord calf.

Long. Let's part the word. 290

Kath. No, I'll not be your half.

Take all and wean it; it may prove an ox.

Long. Look how you butt yourself in these sharp mocks!

Will you give horns, chaste lady? Do not so. 295

Kath. Then die a calf, before your horns do grow.

Long. One word in private with you ere I die.

Kath. Bleat softly, then; the butcher hears you cry.

[*They converse apart.*]

Boy. The tongues of mocking wenches are as keen

As is the razor's edge invisible, 300

Cutting a smaller hair than may be seen,

Above the sense of sense; so sensible

303. **conference:** discourse; **conceits:** fancies; inventive powers.

308. **dry-beaten:** battered but not bloody.

315. **Well-liking:** plump.

321. **cases:** a quibble on "masks."

323. **swear himself out of all suit:** i.e., urge his love suit with so many vows that he exhausted everything he could say and made himself ridiculous.

327. **trow:** know.

331. **statute caps:** ordinary citizens were required by statute to wear woolen caps of English manufacture on Sundays and holidays. This statute was enacted to help the capmakers.

Seemeth their conference; their conceits have wings,
Fleeter than arrows, bullets, wind, thought, swifter
things. 305

Ros. Not one word more, my maids; break off, break off.

Ber. By heaven, all dry-beaten with pure scoff!

King. Farewell, mad wenches; you have simple wits. *Exeunt [King, Lords, and Blackamoors].* 310

Prin. Twenty adieus, my frozen Muscovites.
Are these the breed of wits so wondered at?

Boy. Tapers they are, with your sweet breaths puffed out.

Ros. Well-liking wits they have; gross, gross; fat, fat. 315

Prin. O poverty in wit! kingly-poor flout!
Will they not, think you, hang themselves tonight?
Or ever but in vizards show their faces?
This pert Berowne was out of countenance quite. 320

Ros. They were all in lamentable cases!
The King was weeping-ripe for a good word.

Prin. Berowne did swear himself out of all suit.

Mar. Dumaine was at my service, and his sword.
"No point," quoth I; my servant straight was mute. 325

Kath. Lord Longaville said I came o'er his heart;
And trow you what he called me?

Prin. Qualm, perhaps.

Kath. Yes, in good faith.

Prin. Go, sickness as thou art! 330

Ros. Well, better wits have worn plain statute caps.
But will you hear? The King is my love sworn.

349. **damask . . . commixture:** i.e., mingled red and white complexion like a damask rose.

350. **vailing:** lowering; i.e., removing.

A Russian ambassador. From Cesare Vecellio, *Habiti antichi et moderni di tutto il mondo* (1598)

Prin. And quick Berowne hath plighted faith to me.
Kath. And Longaville was for my service born. 335
Mar. Dumaine is mine, as sure as bark on tree.
Boy. Madam, and pretty mistresses, give ear:
Immediately they will again be here
In their own shapes; for it can never be
They will digest this harsh indignity. 340
Prin. Will they return?
Boy. They will, they will, God knows,
And leap for joy, though they are lame with blows;
Therefore, change favors, and, when they repair,
Blow like sweet roses in this summer air. 345
Prin. How blow? how blow? Speak to be understood.
Boy. Fair ladies masked are roses in their bud:
Dismasked, their damask sweet commixture shown,
Are angels vailing clouds, or roses blown. 350
Prin. Avaunt, perplexity! What shall we do
If they return in their own shapes to woo?
Ros. Good madam, if by me you'll be advised,
Let's mock them still, as well known as disguised.
Let us complain to them what fools were here, 355
Disguised like Muscovites, in shapeless gear;
And wonder what they were, and to what end
Their shallow shows and prologue vilely penned,
And their rough carriage so ridiculous,
Should be presented at our tent to us. 360
Boy. Ladies, withdraw; the gallants are at hand.
Prin. Whip to our tents, as roes run o'er the land.

372. **wakes:** church festivals; **wassails:** revels.

377. **'A can carve:** contemporary slang meaning that he can please the ladies.

380. **tables:** backgammon.

382. **mean:** tenor part.

383. **Mend:** outdo.

A French dandy. From Cesare Vecellio, *Habiti antichi et moderni di tutto il mondo* (1598)

Exeunt [Princess, Rosaline, Katharine, and Maria].

[Re-]enter the King, Berowne, Longaville, and Dumaine, [in their proper habits].

King. Fair sir, God save you! Where's the Princess?
Boy. Gone to her tent. Please it your Majesty
Command me any service to her thither? 365
King. That she vouchsafe me audience for one word.
Boy. I will; and so will she, I know, my lord. *Exit.*
Ber. This fellow pecks up wit as pigeons pease,
And utters it again when God doth please. 370
He is wit's peddler, and retails his wares
At wakes, and wassails, meetings, markets, fairs;
And we that sell by gross, the Lord doth know,
Have not the grace to grace it with such show.
This gallant pins the wenches on his sleeve; 375
Had he been Adam, he had tempted Eve.
'A can carve too, and lisp; why, this is he
That kissed his hand away in courtesy;
This is the ape of form, Monsieur the Nice,
That, when he plays at tables, chides the dice 380
In honorable terms; nay, he can sing
A mean most meanly; and in ushering,
Mend him who can. The ladies call him sweet;
The stairs, as he treads on them, kiss his feet.
This is the flower that smiles on every one, 385
To show his teeth as white as whale's bone;

388. **Pay him the due of:** acknowledge him to be.

404. **virtue:** power.

405. **nickname:** miscall.

And consciences that will not die in debt
Pay him the due of "honey-tongued Boyet."
King. A blister on his sweet tongue, with my heart,
That put Armado's page out of his part! 390

[Re-]enter the Princess, Rosaline, Maria, and Katharine, [and Boyet].

Ber. See where it comes! Behavior, what wert thou
Till this madman showed thee? And what art thou now?
King. All hail, sweet madam, and fair time of day!
Prin. "Fair" in "all hail" is foul, as I conceive. 395
King. Construe my speeches better, if you may.
Prin. Then wish me better; I will give you leave.
King. We came to visit you, and purpose now
To lead you to our court; vouchsafe it then.
Prin. This field shall hold me, and so hold your vow: 400
Nor God, nor I, delights in perjured men.
King. Rebuke me not for that which you provoke.
The virtue of your eye must break my oath.
Prin. You nickname virtue: "vice" you should have spoke; 405
For virtue's office never breaks men's troth.
Now by my maiden honor, yet as pure
As the unsullied lily, I protest,
A world of torments though I should endure, 410
I would not yield to be your house's guest;
So much I hate a breaking cause to be
Of heavenly oaths vowed with integrity.

418. **mess:** i.e., quartet; see IV.[iii.] 229.

423. **to the manner of the days:** in accordance with present custom.

428. **happy:** felicitous; appropriate.

432-34. **when we greet,/With eyes best seeing, heaven's fiery eye,/By light we lose light:** when we encounter with wide-open eyes the full glory of the sun the dazzling light blinds us.

King. O, you have lived in desolation here,
Unseen, unvisited, much to our shame. 415
Prin. Not so, my lord; it is not so, I swear;
We have had pastimes here, and pleasant game;
A mess of Russians left us but of late.
King. How, madam! Russians!
Prin. Ay, in truth, my lord; 420
Trim gallants, full of courtship and of state.
Ros. Madam, speak true. It is not so, my lord.
My lady, to the manner of the days,
In courtesy gives undeserving praise.
We four indeed confronted were with four 425
In Russian habit; here they stayed an hour
And talked apace; and in that hour, my lord,
They did not bless us with one happy word.
I dare not call them fools; but this I think,
When they are thirsty, fools would fain have drink. 430
Ber. This jest is dry to me. Gentle sweet,
Your wit makes wise things foolish; when we greet,
With eyes best seeing, heaven's fiery eye,
By light we lose light; your capacity
Is of that nature that to your huge store 435
Wise things seem foolish and rich things but poor.
Ros. This proves you wise and rich, for, in my eye—
Ber. I am a fool, and full of poverty.
Ros. But that you take what doth to you belong,
It were a fault to snatch words from my tongue. 440
Ber. O, I am yours, and all that I possess.
Ros. All the fool mine?
Ber. I cannot give you less.
Ros. Which of the vizards was it that you wore?

463. **wish:** request; entreat.
464. **habit:** clothing; **wait:** dance attendance.
467. **friend:** ladylove.
470. **spruce:** elegant.

Ber. Where? when? what vizard? Why demand you this? 445

Ros. There, then, that vizard; that superfluous case
That hid the worse and showed the better face.

King. We were descried; they'll mock us now downright. 450

Dum. Let us confess, and turn it to a jest.

Prin. Amazed, my lord? Why looks your Highness sad?

Ros. Help, hold his brows! he'll swoon! Why look you pale? 455
Seasick, I think, coming from Muscovy.

Ber. Thus pour the stars down plagues for perjury.
Can any face of brass hold longer out?
Here stand I, lady—dart thy skill at me,
Bruise me with scorn, confound me with a flout, 460
Thrust thy sharp wit quite through my ignorance,
Cut me to pieces with thy keen conceit;
And I will wish thee never more to dance,
Nor never more in Russian habit wait.
O, never will I trust to speeches penned, 465
Nor to the motion of a schoolboy's tongue,
Nor never come in vizard to my friend,
Nor woo in rhyme, like a blind harper's song.
Taffeta phrases, silken terms precise,
Three-piled hyperboles, spruce affectation, 470
Figures pedantical—these summer flies
Have blown me full of maggot ostentation.
I do forswear them; and I here protest,
By this white glove—how white the hand, God knows!— 475

477. **russet . . . kersey:** coarse, homespun fabrics; i.e., plain and down-to-earth.

480. **"sans":** if he is going to speak plainly, **sans** is too fancy a word.

484. **"Lord have mercy on us":** an inscription put on dwellings to indicate the presence of the plague within.

487. **visited:** afflicted with sickness.

488. **the Lord's tokens:** spots indicating the plague. Berowne is punning. The Lord's tokens he sees are the "fairings" given to the ladies earlier.

492. **stand forfeit, being those that sue:** Rosaline takes **sue** in the legal sense and protests that the one who brings a suit is not the one who pays a penalty.

493. **have to do with:** that is, disagree with.

502. **well advised:** aware of what you were doing; sane.

Henceforth my wooing mind shall be expressed
In russet yeas, and honest kersey noes.
And, to begin, wench—so God help me, law!—
My love to thee is sound, sans crack or flaw.
Ros. Sans "sans," I pray you. 480
Ber. Yet I have a trick
Of the old rage; bear with me, I am sick;
I'll leave it by degrees. Soft, let us see—
Write "Lord have mercy on us" on those three;
They are infected; in their hearts it lies; 485
They have the plague, and caught it of your eyes.
These lords are visited; you are not free,
For the Lord's tokens on you do I see.
Prin. No, they are free that gave these tokens to us.
Ber. Our states are forfeit; seek not to undo us. 490
Ros. It is not so; for how can this be true,
That you stand forfeit, being those that sue?
Ber. Peace! for I will not have to do with you.
Ros. Nor shall not, if I do as I intend.
Ber. Speak for yourselves; my wit is at an end. 495
King. Teach us, sweet madam, for our rude transgression
Some fair excuse.
Prin. The fairest is confession.
Were not you here but even now, disguised? 500
King. Madam, I was.
Prin. And were you well advised?
King. I was, fair madam.
Prin. When you then were here,
What did you whisper in your lady's ear? 505

512. **force not to forswear:** think nothing of being forsworn. **Force** is used in the sense of having regard for, valuing.

532. **remit:** surrender.

533. **consent:** plot.

535. **dash it like a Christmas comedy:** make merry at our expense in the same way spectators traditionally chaffed the performers of farces performed on holidays.

536. **pleaseman:** currier of favor; **zany:** clown.

King. That more than all the world I did respect her.

Prin. When she shall challenge this, you will reject her.

King. Upon mine honor, no. 510

Prin. Peace, peace, forbear;
Your oath once broke, you force not to forswear.

King. Despise me when I break this oath of mine.

Prin. I will; and therefore keep it. Rosaline,
What did the Russian whisper in your ear? 515

Ros. Madam, he swore that he did hold me dear
As precious eyesight, and did value me
Above this world; adding thereto, moreover,
That he would wed me, or else die my lover.

Prin. God give thee joy of him! The noble lord 520
Most honorably doth uphold his word.

King. What mean you, madam? By my life, my troth,
I never swore this lady such an oath.

Ros. By heaven, you did; and, to confirm it plain, 525
You gave me this; but take it, sir, again.

King. My faith and this the Princess I did give;
I knew her by this jewel on her sleeve.

Prin. Pardon me, sir, this jewel did she wear;
And Lord Berowne, I thank him, is my dear. 530
What, will you have me, or your pearl again?

Ber. Neither of either; I remit both twain.
I see the trick on't: here was a consent,
Knowing aforehand of our merriment,
To dash it like a Christmas comedy. 535
Some carrytale, some pleaseman, some slight zany,

537. **trencher knight:** one famed for his deeds at meals; **Dick:** Jack; knave.

538. **smiles his cheek in years:** smiles so much that his face wrinkles prematurely.

545. **Much upon this it is:** this must be pretty much what happened.

547. **know my lady's foot by the squire:** i.e., know exactly what will please the ladies. A **squire** is a foot rule.

548. **laugh upon the apple of her eye:** jest with her familiarly.

552. **smock:** woman's undergarment.

556. **brave:** splendid; **manage:** exercise (normally, of horsemanship); **career:** headlong gallop. Boyet is sneering at Berowne's long tirade.

557. **tilting:** thrusting with his wit; **straight:** at once.

Some mumblenews, some trencher knight, some Dick,
That smiles his cheek in years and knows the trick
To make my lady laugh when she's disposed,
Told our intents before; which once disclosed, 540
The ladies did change favors; and then we,
Following the signs, wooed but the sign of she.
Now, to our perjury to add more terror,
We are again forsworn in will and error.
Much upon this it is; [*To Boyet*] and might not you 545
Forestall our sport, to make us thus untrue?
Do not you know my lady's foot by the squire,
And laugh upon the apple of her eye?
And stand between her back, sir, and the fire,
Holding a trencher, jesting merrily? 550
You put our page out. Go, you are allowed;
Die when you will, a smock shall be your shroud.
You leer upon me, do you? There's an eye
Wounds like a leaden sword.

Boy. Full merrily 555
Hath this brave manage, this career, been run.

Ber. Lo, he is tilting straight! Peace; I have done.

Enter Costard.

Welcome, pure wit! Thou partst a fair fray.

Cost. O Lord, sir, they would know
Whether the three Worthies shall come in or no? 560

Ber. What, are there but three?

Cost. No, sir; but it is vara fine,
For every one pursents three.

Ber. And three times thrice is nine.

565. under correction: an apology for seeming to disagree.

567. You cannot beg us: i.e., we cannot be proved fools. The crown had rights over the lands and the guardianship of minors who inherited large estates. Wealthy idiots came under the same provision. An applicant for the guardianship of such a person would "beg" him in the Court of Wards.

580. Pompion: colloquial for "pumpkin," often applied satirically to a big man.

Cost. Not so, sir; under correction, sir, I hope it is not so. 565
You cannot beg us, sir, I can assure you, sir; we know what we know;
I hope, sir, three times thrice, sir—

Ber. Is not nine. 570

Cost. Under correction, sir, we know whereuntil it doth amount.

Ber. By Jove, I always took three threes for nine.

Cost. O Lord, sir, it were pity you should get your living by reck'ning, sir. 575

Ber. How much is it?

Cost. O Lord, sir, the parties themselves, the actors, sir, will show whereuntil it doth amount. For mine own part, I am, as they say, but to perfect one man in one poor man, Pompion the Great, sir. 580

Ber. Art thou one of the Worthies?

Cost. It pleased them to think me worthy of Pompey the Great; for mine own part, I know not the degree of the Worthy, but I am to stand for him.

Ber. Go, bid them prepare. 585

Cost. We will turn it finely off, sir; we will take some care. *Exit.*

King. Berowne, they will shame us; let them not approach.

Ber. We are shameproof, my lord, and 'tis some policy 590
To have one show worse than the King's and his company.

King. I say they shall not come.

Prin. Nay, my good lord, let me o'errule you now. 595

602. **Anointed:** "Anointed one." Armado is addressing the King.

606. **God His making:** an old colloquial form of the possessive.

610. **fortuna de la guerra:** the fortunes of war.

611. **couplement:** couple.

That sport best pleases that doth least know how;
Where zeal strives to content, and the contents
Dies in the zeal of that which it presents.
Their form confounded makes most form in mirth,
When great things laboring perish in their birth. 600

Ber. A right description of our sport, my lord.

Enter Armado.

Arm. Anointed, I implore so much expense of thy royal sweet breath as will utter a brace of words.

[*Converses apart with the King, and delivers a paper.*]

Prin. Doth this man serve God?

Ber. Why ask you? 605

Prin. 'A speaks not like a man of God His making.

Arm. That is all one, my fair, sweet, honey monarch; for, I protest, the schoolmaster is exceeding fantastical; too too vain, too too vain; but we will put it, as they say, to *fortuna de la guerra*. I wish you 610 the peace of mind, most royal couplement! *Exit.*

King. Here is like to be a good presence of Worthies. He presents Hector of Troy; the swain, Pompey the Great; the parish curate, Alexander; Armado's page, Hercules; the pedant, Judas Mac- 615 cabæus.
And if these four Worthies in their first show thrive,
These four will change habits and present the other
five.

Ber. There is five in the first show. 620

King. You are deceived, 'tis not so.

622. **hedge priest:** an illiterate priest of inferior order.

624. **Abate throw at novum:** except for a throw at "novem quinque" (a dice game played by five persons, the two principal throws being nine and five). Here they have five persons standing for Nine Worthies.

631. **libbard:** leopard. An allusion to Pompey's crest.

638. **targe:** target; shield.

Ber. The pedant, the braggart, the hedge priest, the fool, and the boy:
Abate throw at novum, and the whole world again
Cannot pick out five such, take each one in his vein. 625

King. The ship is under sail, and here she comes amain.

Enter [Costard, armed for] Pompey.

Cost. "I Pompey am—"

Ber. You lie, you are not he.

Cost. "I Pompey am—" 630

Boy. With libbard's head on knee.

Ber. Well said, old mocker; I must needs be friends with thee.

Cost. "I Pompey am, Pompey surnamed the Big—"

Dum. The "Great." 635

Cost. It is "Great," sir.
"Pompey surnamed the Great,
That oft in field, with targe and shield, did make my foe to sweat;
And traveling along this coast, I here am come by chance, 640
And lay my arms before the legs of this sweet lass of France."
If your ladyship would say, "Thanks, Pompey," I had done. 645

Prin. Great thanks, great Pompey.

Cost. 'Tis not so much worth; but I hope I was perfect. I made a little fault in "Great."

655. **scutcheon:** shield bearing a coat-of-arms; **plain:** plainly.

656-57. **it stands too right:** Alexander was described in North's Plutarch as inclining his neck somewhat to the left.

658-59. **Your nose smells "no" in this, most tender-smelling knight:** Plutarch reported Alexander to have a sweet-smelling body—which the curate lacks.

671-72. **painted cloth:** painted hangings showing scenes from mythology and romance were used for decoration in homes. The Nine Worthies was a favorite subject for such cloths; **Your lion, that holds his poleax sitting on a closestool:** Costard's comic description of the arms of Alexander as described in a contemporary treatise on heraldry: a lion seated in a chair holding a battleax. A **closestool** is a box containing a chamber pot.

673. **Ajax:** a pun, very popular in Elizabethan times, resting on the pronunciation of **Ajax** as "a-jakes" (privy).

Alexander the Great. From Paolo Giovio, *Elogia veris clarorum virorum* (1589)

Ber. My hat to a halfpenny, Pompey proves the best Worthy. 650

Enter Sir Nathaniel, for Alexander.

Nath. "When in the world I lived, I was the world's commander;
By east, west, north, and south, I spread my conquering might.
My scutcheon plain declares that I am Alisander—" 655

Boy. Your nose says, no, you are not; for it stands too right.

Ber. Your nose smells "no" in this, most tender-smelling knight.

Prin. The conqueror is dismayed. Proceed, good Alexander. 660

Nath. "When in the world I lived, I was the world's commander—"

Boy. Most true, 'tis right, you were so, Alisander.

Ber. Pompey the Great! 665

Cost. Your servant, and Costard.

Ber. Take away the conqueror, take away Alisander.

Cost. [*To Sir Nathaniel*] O, sir, you have overthrown Alisander the conqueror! You will be scraped 670 out of the painted cloth for this. Your lion, that holds his poleax sitting on a closestool, will be given to Ajax; he will be the ninth Worthy. A conqueror and afeared to speak! Run away for shame, Alisander.

Exit Nathaniel.

There, an't shall please you, a foolish mild man; an 675

679. **o'erparted:** given a part too great for his ability.

683. **Cerberus:** the watchdog of Hades, which Hercules brought up from the nether region as his eleventh labor. Hercules is depicted in emblem books choking the dog, which may have given the impression that he killed Cerberus; **canis:** dog.

685. **manus:** hand.

686. **Quoniam:** seeing that.

687. **Ergo:** therefore.

694. **A kissing traitor:** a reference to the Judas kiss. **Clipt** also means "kissed"; **How, art thou proved Judas:** there, have I not proved you to be Judas?

699. **elder:** traditionally the tree on which Judas hanged himself.

704. **citternhead:** a cittern (or cithern) was a type of guitar on the head of which was often carved a grotesque face.

Hercules and Cerberus. From Gabriel Simeoni, *La vita et Metamorfoseo d'Ovidio* (1559)

honest man, look you, and soon dashed. He is a marvelous good neighbor, faith, and a very good bowler; but for Alisander—alas! you see how 'tis—a little o'erparted. But there are Worthies a-coming will speak their mind in some other sort. 680

Prin. Stand aside, good Pompey.

Enter Holofernes, for Judas; and Moth, for Hercules.

Hol. "Great Hercules is presented by this imp,
Whose club killed Cerberus, that three-headed *canis;*
And when he was a babe, a child, a shrimp,
Thus did he strangle serpents in his *manus.* 685
Quoniam he seemeth in minority,
Ergo I come with this apology."
Keep some state in thy exit, and vanish. *Exit Moth.*
"Judas I am—"

Dum. A Judas! 690

Hol. Not Iscariot, sir.
"Judas I am, ycliped Maccabæus."

Dum. Judas Maccabæus clipt is plain Judas.

Ber. A kissing traitor. How, art thou proved Judas?

Hol. "Judas I am—" 695

Dum. The more shame for you, Judas!

Hol. What mean you, sir?

Boy. To make Judas hang himself.

Hol. Begin, sir; you are my elder.

Ber. Well followed: Judas was hanged on an elder. 700

Hol. I will not be put out of countenance.

Ber. Because thou hast no face.

Hol. What is this?

Boy. A cittern-head.

705. **bodkin:** a word for a small dagger and a lady's hairpin, both of which commonly had carved heads.

708. **falchion:** sword.

710. **half-cheek:** profile.

712. **worn in the cap of a toothdrawer:** itinerant toothdrawers, as part of their costume, wore brooches in their hats.

730. **by:** to.

732. **Troyan:** i.e., just another one of the boys. **Troyan** was used to mean "good fellow."

Judas Maccabæus. From *Chronologie et sommaire des souverains, pontifes, anciens péres* (1622)

Dum. The head of a bodkin. 705

Ber. A death's face in a ring.

Long. The face of an old Roman coin, scarce seen.

Boy. The pommel of Cæsar's falchion.

Dum. The carved-bone face on a flask.

Ber. Saint George's half-cheek in a brooch. 710

Dum. Ay, and in a brooch of lead.

Ber. Ay, and worn in the cap of a toothdrawer. And now, forward; for we have put thee in countenance.

Hol. You have put me out of countenance.

Ber. False: we have given thee faces. 715

Hol. But you have outfaced them all.

Ber. An thou wert a lion we would do so.

Boy. Therefore, as he is an ass, let him go.
And so adieu, sweet Jude! Nay, why dost thou stay?

Dum. For the latter end of his name. 720

Ber. For the ass to the Jude; give it him—Jud-as, away!

Hol. This is not generous, not gentle, not humble.

Boy. A light for Monsieur Judas! It grows dark, he may stumble. [*Holofernes retires.*] 725

Prin. Alas, poor Maccabæus, how hath he been baited!

Enter Armado, [for Hector].

Ber. Hide thy head, Achilles; here comes Hector in arms.

Dum. Though my mocks come home by me, I will now be merry. 730

King. Hector was but a Troyan in respect of this.

734. **clean-timbered:** well-built.

736. **calf:** a pun on another meaning: "fool."

737. **indued:** endowed.

739. **He's a god or a painter; for he makes faces:** a proverbial idea.

740. **armipotent:** "mighty in arms" from the Latin *armipotentem*.

742. **gilt:** glazed with egg, probably as a preservative.

748. **Ilion:** Troy.

749. **so breathed:** of such endurance.

Boy. But is this Hector?

Dum. I think Hector was not so clean-timbered.

Long. His leg is too big for Hector's. 735

Dum. More calf, certain.

Boy. No; he is best indued in the small.

Ber. This cannot be Hector.

Dum. He's a god or a painter; for he makes faces.

Arm. "The armipotent Mars, of lances the almighty, 740
Gave Hector a gift—"

Dum. A gilt nutmeg.

Ber. A lemon.

Long. Stuck with cloves.

Dum. No, cloven. 745

Arm. Peace!
"The armipotent Mars, of lances the almighty,
Gave Hector a gift, the heir of Ilion;
A man so breathed that certain he would fight; yea,
From morn till night out of his pavilion. 750
I am that flower—"

Dum. That mint.

Long. That columbine.

Arm. Sweet Lord Longaville, rein thy tongue.

Long. I must rather give it the rein, for it runs 755
against Hector.

Dum. Ay, and Hector's a greyhound.

Arm. The sweet warman is dead and rotten; sweet chucks, beat not the bones of the buried; when he breathed, he was a man. But I will forward with my 760
device. [*To the Princess*] Sweet royalty, bestow on me the sense of hearing.

Berowne steps forth [*and speaks to Costard*].

775. **infamonize:** charge with infamous behavior.

785. **Ates:** Ate was a daughter of the Greek goddess Eris (Discord), whose function was to incite men to rashness.

791-92. **a northern man:** a thief of the Border regions, whose weapon was usually a long staff.

Hector and Ajax. From Lodovido Dolce, *Le trasformationi* (1570)

Prin. Speak, brave Hector; we are much delighted.
Arm. I do adore thy sweet Grace's slipper.
Boy. [*Aside to Dumaine*] Loves her by the foot. 765
Dum. [*Aside to Boyet*] He may not by the yard.
Arm. "This Hector far surmounted Hannibal—
The party is gone—"
Cost. Fellow Hector, she is gone; she is two months on her way. 770
Arm. What meanest thou?
Cost. Faith, unless you play the honest Troyan, the poor wench is cast away. She's quick; the child brags in her belly already; 'tis yours.
Arm. Dost thou infamonize me among potentates? 775 Thou shalt die.
Cost. Then shall Hector be whipped for Jaquenetta that is quick by him, and hanged for Pompey that is dead by him.
Dum. Most rare Pompey! 780
Boy. Renowned Pompey!
Ber. Greater than Great! Great, great, great Pompey! Pompey the Huge!
Dum. Hector trembles.
Ber. Pompey is moved. More Ates, more Ates! Stir 785 them on! stir them on!
Dum. Hector will challenge him.
Ber. Ay, if 'a have no more man's blood in his belly than will sup a flea.
Arm. By the North Pole, I do challenge thee. 790
Cost. I will not fight with a pole, like a northern man; I'll slash; I'll do it by the sword. I bepray you, let me borrow my arms again.

797. **take you a buttonhole lower:** remove your outer garment. The phrase also meant to expose to humiliation.

807. **woolward:** i.e., with wool next the skin.

Dum. Room for the incensed Worthies!

Cost. I'll do it in my shirt. 795

Dum. Most resolute Pompey!

Moth. Master, let me take you a buttonhole lower. Do you not see Pompey is uncasing for the combat? What mean you? You will lose your reputation.

Arm. Gentlemen and soldiers, pardon me; I will 800 not combat in my shirt.

Dum. You may not deny it: Pompey hath made the challenge.

Arm. Sweet bloods, I both may and will.

Ber. What reason have you for't? 805

Arm. The naked truth of it is: I have no shirt; I go woolward for penance.

Boy. True, and it was enjoined him in Rome for want of linen; since when, I'll be sworn, he wore none but a dishclout of Jaquenetta's, and that 'a wears 810 next his heart for a favor.

Enter a messenger, Monsieur Marcade.

Marc. God save you, madam!

Prin. Welcome, Marcade;
But that thou interruptest our merriment.

Marc. I am sorry, madam; for the news I bring 815
Is heavy in my tongue. The King your father—

Prin. Dead, for my life!

Marc. Even so; my tale is told.

Ber. Worthies, away! the scene begins to cloud.

Arm. For mine own part, I breathe free breath. 820

821-22. seen the day of wrong through the little hole of discretion: proverbial. Armado means that he is not such a fool that he fails to see the wrong being done him.

830. liberal: unrestrained; overfree.

832-33. your gentleness/Was guilty of it: your courteous tolerance was responsible for our daring to do so.

834. nimble: Theobald's correction of "humble" in the early texts.

837-38. The extreme parts of time extremely forms/All causes to . . . his speed: shortness of time compels quick decision.

839. at his very loose: i.e., at the instant Time lets fly its arrow.

843. convince: establish.

I have seen the day of wrong through the little hole of discretion, and I will right myself like a soldier.

Exeunt Worthies.

King. How fares your Majesty?

Prin. Boyet, prepare; I will away tonight.

King. Madam, not so; I do beseech you stay. 825

Prin. Prepare, I say. I thank you, gracious lords,
For all your fair endeavors, and entreat,
Out of a new-sad soul, that you vouchsafe
In your rich wisdom to excuse or hide
The liberal opposition of our spirits, 830
If overboldly we have borne ourselves
In the converse of breath—your gentleness
Was guilty of it. Farewell, worthy lord.
A heavy heart bears not a nimble tongue.
Excuse me so, coming too short of thanks 835
For my great suit so easily obtained.

King. The extreme parts of time extremely forms
All causes to the purpose of his speed;
And often at his very loose decides
That which long process could not arbitrate. 840
And though the mourning brow of progeny
Forbid the smiling courtesy of love
The holy suit which fain it would convince,
Yet, since love's argument was first on foot,
Let not the cloud of sorrow justle it 845
From what it purposed; since to wail friends lost
Is not by much so wholesome-profitable
As to rejoice at friends but newly found.

Prin. I understand you not; my griefs are double.

852. **badges:** evidences, i.e., the actions which Berowne then enumerates.

858. **strains:** impulses.

859. **wanton:** playful; **skipping and vain:** capricious and frivolous.

861. **straying:** fleeting.

864. **parti-coated:** motley; foolish.

868. **Suggested:** tempted.

879. **bombast:** padding; something to fill out or pass the time.

Ber. Honest plain words best pierce the ear of grief; 850
And by these badges understand the King:
For your fair sakes have we neglected time,
Played foul play with our oaths; your beauty, ladies,
Hath much deformed us, fashioning our humors 855
Even to the opposed end of our intents;
And what in us hath seemed ridiculous,
As love is full of unbefitting strains,
All wanton as a child, skipping and vain;
Formed by the eye and therefore, like the eye, 860
Full of straying shapes, of habits, and of forms,
Varying in subjects as the eye doth roll
To every varied object in his glance;
Which parti-coated presence of loose love
Put on by us, if in your heavenly eyes 865
Have misbecomed our oaths and gravities,
Those heavenly eyes that look into these faults
Suggested us to make. Therefore, ladies,
Our love being yours, the error that love makes
Is likewise yours. We to ourselves prove false, 870
By being once false forever to be true
To those that make us both—fair ladies, you.
And even that falsehood, in itself a sin,
Thus purifies itself and turns to grace.

Prin. We have received your letters, full of love; 875
Your favors, the ambassadors of love;
And, in our maiden council, rated them
At courtship, pleasant jest, and courtesy,
As bombast and as lining to the time;
But more devout than this in our respects 880

886. **quote:** interpret.
892. **dear:** forgivable.
898. **signs:** i.e., of the Zodiac.
902. **weeds:** garments.
904. **last:** remain unchanged.
906. **by these deserts:** on the basis of these worthy actions.

Have we not been; and therefore met your loves
In their own fashion, like a merriment.

Dum. Our letters, madam, showed much more than jest.

Long. So did our looks. 885

Ros. We did not quote them so.

King. Now, at the latest minute of the hour,
Grant us your loves.

Prin. A time, methinks, too short
To make a world-without-end bargain in. 890
No, no, my lord, your Grace is perjured much,
Full of dear guiltiness; and therefore this—
If for my love, as there is no such cause,
You will do aught—this shall you do for me:
Your oath I will not trust; but go with speed 895
To some forlorn and naked hermitage,
Remote from all the pleasures of the world;
There stay until the twelve celestial signs
Have brought about the annual reckoning.
If this austere insociable life 900
Change not your offer made in heat of blood,
If frosts and fasts, hard lodging and thin weeds,
Nip not the gaudy blossoms of your love,
But that it bear this trial, and last love,
Then, at the expiration of the year, 905
Come, challenge me, challenge me by these deserts;
And, by this virgin palm now kissing thine,
I will be thine; and, till that instant, shut
My woeful self up in a mourning house,
Raining the tears of lamentation 910
For the remembrance of my father's death.

913. **entitled in:** holding a legal claim to.

915. **flatter up these powers of mine with rest:** coddle myself.

918-23. **And . . . sick:** this material may have been meant for deletion. Berowne and Rosaline have a longer dialogue below.

919. **your sins are racked:** you are being made to suffer for your sins.

920. **attaint with:** attainted (convicted) of.

930. **smooth-faced:** clean-shaven, and plausible (but untrustworthy).

937. **friend:** lover.

938. **stay:** wait.

940. **Studies:** muses; meditates.

If this thou do deny, let our hands part,
Neither entitled in the other's heart.

King. If this, or more than this, I would deny,
To flatter up these powers of mine with rest, 915
The sudden hand of death close up mine eye!
Hence hermit then, my heart is in thy breast.

Ber. And what to me, my love? and what to me?

Ros. You must be purged too; your sins are racked;
You are attaint with faults and perjury; 920
Therefore, if you my favor mean to get,
A twelvemonth shall you spend, and never rest,
But seek the weary beds of people sick.

Dum. But what to me, my love? but what to me?
A wife? 925

Kath. A beard, fair health, and honesty;
With threefold love I wish you all these three.

Dum. O, shall I say I thank you, gentle wife?

Kath. Not so, my lord; a twelvemonth and a day
I'll mark no words that smooth-faced wooers say. 930
Come when the King doth to my lady come;
Then, if I have much love, I'll give you some.

Dum. I'll serve thee true and faithfully till then.

Kath. Yet swear not, lest ye be forsworn again.

Long. What says Maria? 935

Mar. At the twelvemonth's end
I'll change my black gown for a faithful friend.

Long. I'll stay with patience; but the time is long.

Mar. The liker you; few taller are so young.

Ber. Studies my lady? Mistress, look on me; 940
Behold the window of my heart, mine eye,

945. **large:** loose.
946. **replete with:** abundantly supplied with.
947. **comparisons:** satirical comments.
948. **estates:** classes; sorts.

What humble suit attends thy answer there.
Impose some service on me for thy love.
Ros. Oft have I heard of you, my Lord Berowne,
Before I saw you; and the world's large tongue 945
Proclaims you for a man replete with mocks,
Full of comparisons and wounding flouts,
Which you on all estates will execute
That lie within the mercy of your wit.
To weed this wormwood from your fruitful brain, 950
And therewithal to win me, if you please,
Without the which I am not to be won,
You shall this twelvemonth term from day to day
Visit the speechless sick, and still converse
With groaning wretches; and your task shall be, 955
With all the fierce endeavor of your wit,
To enforce the pained impotent to smile.
Ber. To move wild laughter in the throat of death?
It cannot be; it is impossible;
Mirth cannot move a soul in agony. 960
Ros. Why, that's the way to choke a gibing spirit,
Whose influence is begot of that loose grace
Which shallow laughing hearers give to fools.
A jest's prosperity lies in the ear
Of him that hears it, never in the tongue 965
Of him that makes it; then, if sickly ears,
Deafed with the clamors of their own dear groans,
Will hear your idle scorns, continue then,
And I will have you and that fault withal.
But if they will not, throw away that spirit, 970
And I shall find you empty of that fault,
Right joyful of your reformation.

977. bring: escort.

Ber. A twelvemonth? Well, befall what will befall,
I'll jest a twelvemonth in an hospital.
Prin. [*To the King*] Ay, sweet my lord, and so I take my leave. 975
King. No, madam; we will bring you on your way.
Ber. Our wooing doth not end like an old play:
Jack hath not Jill. These ladies' courtesy
Might well have made our sport a comedy. 980
King. Come, sir, it wants a twelvemonth and a day,
And then 'twill end.
Ber. That's too long for a play.

[Re-]enter Armado.

Arm. Sweet Majesty, vouchsafe me—
Prin. Was not that Hector? 985
Dum. The worthy knight of Troy.
Arm. I will kiss thy royal finger, and take leave. I am a votary: I have vowed to Jaquenetta to hold the plow for her sweet love three year. But, most esteemed greatness, will you hear the dialogue that 990 the two learned men have compiled in praise of the Owl and the Cuckoo? It should have followed in the end of our show.
King. Call them forth quickly; we will do so.
Arm. Holla! approach. 995

Enter All.

This side is Hiems, Winter; this Ver, the Spring—the one maintained by the Owl, the other by the Cuckoo. Ver, begin.

1000. **lady smocks:** a common English wildflower, *cardamine pratensis.*

1001. **cuckoo-buds:** probably buttercups.

1010. **turtles:** turtledoves; **tread:** mate.

1021. **ways be foul:** roads are muddy.

The Song

Spring.

When daisies pied and violets blue
And lady smocks all silver-white 1000
And cuckoo-buds of yellow hue
Do paint the meadows with delight,
The cuckoo then on every tree
Mocks married men, for thus sings he:
"Cuckoo; 1005
Cuckoo, cuckoo"–O word of fear,
Unpleasing to a married ear!

When shepherds pipe on oaten straws,
And merry larks are plowman's clocks;
When turtles tread, and rooks and daws, 1010
And maidens bleach their summer smocks;
The cuckoo then on every tree
Mocks married men, for thus sings he:
"Cuckoo;
Cuckoo, cuckoo"–O word of fear, 1015
Unpleasing to a married ear!

Winter.

When icicles hang by the wall,
And Dick the shepherd blows his nail,
And Tom bears logs into the hall,
And milk comes frozen home in pail, 1020
When blood is nipped, and ways be foul,

1024. **keel:** cool, by stirring, skimming, or adding cold liquid.

1026. **saw:** i.e., the moral of his sermon.

1029. **crabs hiss in the bowl:** that is, crab apples simmer in hot punch.

Then nightly sings the staring owl:
"Tu-whit, Tu-who"—A merry note,
While greasy Joan doth keel the pot.

When all aloud the wind doth blow, 1025
  And coughing drowns the parson's saw,
And birds sit brooding in the snow,
  And Marian's nose looks red and raw,
When roasted crabs hiss in the bowl,
Then nightly sings the staring owl: 1030
"Tu-whit, Tu-who"—A merry note,
While greasy Joan doth keel the pot.

Arm. The words of Mercury are harsh after the songs of Apollo. You that way: we this way.

Exeunt omnes.

KEY TO

Famous Lines and Phrases

Make us heirs of all eternity. [*King*–I. i. 7]

The huge army of the world's desires. [*King*–I. i. 10]

Fat paunches have lean pates. [*Longaville*–I. i. 27]

Small have continual plodders ever won,
Save base authority from others' books. [*Berowne*–I. i. 89-90]

Berowne is like an envious sneaping frost
That bites the first-born infants of the spring.
[*King*–I. i. 108-9]

At Christmas I no more desire a rose
Than wish a snow in May's newfangled shows;
But like of each thing that in season grows.
[*Berowne*–I. i. 114-16]

A man of fire-new words. [*Berowne*–I. i. 192]

A child of our grandmother Eve, a female; or, for thy more sweet understanding, a woman. [*Armado*–I. i. 275-77]

Sit thee down, sorrow! [*Costard*–I. i. 325-26]

Love is a familiar; Love is a devil; there is no evil angel but love . . . I am for whole volumes in folio. [*Armado*–I. ii. 171-84]

This wimpled, whining, purblind, wayward boy,
This Signior junior, giant-dwarf, Dan Cupid.
[*Berowne*–III. i. 189-90]

Sonnet. On a day—alack the day!—
Love, whose month is ever May,
Spied a blossom passing fair
Playing in the wanton air. [*Dumaine*–IV. iii. 108-11]

But love, first learned in a lady's eyes,
Lives not alone immured in the brain. . . .
For valor, is not Love a Hercules,
Still climbing trees in the Hesperides?
Subtle as Sphinx; as sweet and musical
As bright Apollo's lute, strung with his hair.
[*Berowne*—IV. iii. 361-77]

For wisdom's sake, a word that all men love.
[*Berowne*—IV. iii. 391]

They have been at a great feast of languages and
stol'n the scraps. [*Moth*—V. i. 36-7]

In the posteriors of this day, which the rude
multitude call the afternoon. [*Armado*—V. i. 85-6]

The tongues of mocking wenches are as keen
As is the razor's edge invisible. [*Boyet*—V. ii. 299-300]

Taffeta phrases, silken terms precise,
Three-piled hyperboles, spruce affectation.
[*Berowne*—V. ii. 469-70]

'A speaks not like a man of God His making.
[*Princess*—V. ii. 606]

A foolish mild man; an honest man, look you, and soon
dashed. He is a marvelous good neighbor, faith,
and a very good bowler. [*Costard*—V. ii. 675-78]

A time, methinks, too short
To make a world-without-end bargain in.
[*Princess*—V. ii. 889-90]

Song. When daisies pied and violets blue . . .
[*Spring*—V. ii. 999-1016]

Song. When icicles hang by the wall . . .
[*Winter*—V. ii. 1017-32]